I0703043

<u>**PRAISE FOR**</u>

<u>**BIRTHDAY PARTY DEMON**</u>

"In *Birthday Party Demon*, Tina's sweet sixteen sleepover turns as sour as green, ectoplasmic vomit. Wendy Dalrymple expertly combines teen friendships, forbidden love, and demonic possession in this nostalgic 90s pink horror romp. You'll want to slap on some Wet n Wild, dust off your Ouija, and join the fun."

-Angela Sylvaine, author of
Frost Bite and *Chopping Spree*

"Dalrymple hosts a sixteenth so scary and sweet, you'll never want the sleepover to end. Friendship, fashion, and fear meld together into a demonic whirlwind that perfectly encapsulates the anxieties of being a teen. This nostalgic foray into the '90s left me wanting to buy inflatable furniture and holy water."

-Stephanie Sanders-Jacob, author of
Pyramidia

"*Birthday Party Demon* delivers! Whether this is your first foray into teen horror, or a nostalgic trip down Fear Street, this book has the chills, creep outs, and chaos you're looking for. Old school thrill seekers will enjoy buddy-reading this book with the next generation of horror fans."

-Joanna Monahan, award-winning author of
Something Better

"Dalrymple delivers a pink horror exorcism you'll be totally bummed to finish!"

-Damien Casey, author of
The Nine Teeth of the River Styx

"A nonstop nostalgic '90s nightmare, *Birthday Party Demon* is a Lisa Frank-tinted thrill ride from beginning to end. I couldn't put it down."

-Robbie Dorman, author of
This Book is Cursed

"*Birthday Party Demon* is a 90s-drenched fashionista nightmare well worth losing yourself in. It's a perfect ode to the very real anxieties of teenagerdom, tightly-paced and scary fun with a demonic candy coating."

-T.T. Madden, author of

The Familialists and *The Cosmic Color*

"*Birthday Party Demon* reads like if your favorite deadite found a creepy, glittery scrunchie, then RSVPed yes to your super sweet sixteen. Dalrymple throws a fun, loud, sparkly party with the best of them."

-William Sterling, author of

String Them Up

An uninvited party guest is about to crash Tina's Sweet Sixteen...

Tina glanced up at Lacey and nearly screamed again, but the sound caught in her throat. Her friend's floating body slowly rotated like a chicken on a rotisserie until Lacey was facing them again. Her hair hung in her face, but it didn't obstruct their view of her eyes. Her entire expression was sinister, a sneer set on her bloodless lips, the color drained from her suntanned skin. But it was the eyes that were most terrifying. They *glowed*.

"Lacey?"

Laughter echoed through the room, dark and sinister. Tina and Eve screamed again as their friend's mouth opened to reveal rows of sharp, shiny teeth.

"There is no Lacey," she said, her voice deep and husky. Inhuman. "Only Zozo."

TOTALLY FREAKED!

Birthday Party
Demon

Wendy Dalrymple

MADAXEMEDIA.COM

Copyright © 2025 by Wendy Dalrymple

All rights reserved.

No part of this publication may be reproduced, distributed, or transmitted in any form or by any means, including photocopying, recording, or other electronic or mechanical methods, without the prior written permission of the publisher, except as permitted by U.S. copyright law. For permission requests, contact info@madaxemedia.com.

The Totally Freaked! series is an original creation of Mad Axe Media.

Book Cover & Interior Design by Joey Powell

Print ISBN: 979-8-9906858-2-6

EBook ISBN: 979-8-9906858-3-3

To Mr. Stine:

Thank you for inspiring generations of spooky young
readers like me.

BIRTHDAY PARTY DEMON

Chapter One

Tina, Lacey and Eve were friends. *Best* friends, to be precise. Since the second grade, the trio of girls did absolutely everything together. From sleepovers to selling Girl Scout cookies, first crushes and first heartbreaks, they were there for each other until the end. But the summer after ninth grade, something seemed to shift in the dynamic of the three best friends. The teens were drifting away from one another thanks to team sports, new friends, and changing interests. Tina was the first to notice that, with the onset of high school, their friend group had begun to unravel.

On the eve of her sixteenth birthday, Tina dragged herself out of bed and padded down the hall toward the kitchen. Her mother, Mary Anne, was dressed in a smart pantsuit for work, her hair perfectly feathered and set with maximum hold hairspray as she stood over the stove. Tina yawned and slid behind the kitchen counter as her mother turned to her with a smile.

"Good morning, sleepyhead."

"Morning."

"Got any plans today?"

"Nope," Tina said. "Nada."

"I bet you thought I forgot," she said. "What do you want to do for your sweet sixteen birthday party this year?"

Tina's mother placed a plate of fried eggs and toast in front of her. The late July morning was already blistering hot and Tina was not even remotely hungry yet. Her stomach flipped as she gazed down at her plate, the gelatinous egg whites and runny yellow yolk glinting and jiggling in the bright sunlight. She pushed the plate away and made a gagging sound.

"Nothing. I'm too old for birthday parties."

"Don't you want to do something with your friends?" Her mother asked. "You could go see a movie or get pizza."

"I don't think Lacey and Eve want to hang out with

me that much anymore."

"Don't be silly. You three have been inseparable since you were eight-years-old."

"Well, we're not little kids anymore. Lacey is super focused on softball and Eve has been hanging out with the goth kids. I don't think I fit into their lives anymore."

Her mother popped her morning pill and swallowed it down before continuing her thought. "I know! What if you all have a sleepover? You three always had the most fun at your sleepovers."

"We're *definitely* too old for sleepovers." Tina groaned. It was like her mother wasn't even listening.

"Christina Louise Martin, you call your friends and invite them over! You've been moping around all summer. I won't let you be a Debbie Downer another moment longer. Now, eat your breakfast."

"Fine."

Tina grabbed her fork and begrudgingly dug into her breakfast. She knew her mother was right, but still, she dreaded making the call. The truth was, it hurt for her to see her friends grow up and move on, but there was something else even bigger than drifting friendships that was bugging her. Tina had a big secret that she couldn't tell her mother or her best friends or anyone, and it was eating her alive.

She finished her breakfast, rinsed her plate and padded to her bedroom, the one place in the world where she felt the most like herself. For her birthday the year before, Tina and her mother had decorated the room to look like a hot pink paradise, complete with posters of all of her favorite singers pinned to the wall. She flopped on her bed as Jewel, Gwen Stefani, Tori Amos, and Mariah Carey stared down at her, gorgeous pop princesses she aspired to be like. With a pit in her stomach, Tina rolled over and grabbed her see-through neon phone and punched in Lacey's number, a series of seven digits she knew by heart.

"Yo." Lacey picked up after the first ring. The sound of snapping bubble gum and rap music beatboxed in Tina's ear. "I was just gonna call you."

"How did you know it was me?"

"My step-dad got caller ID." Lacey snapped her gum and turned down the music. "Hold on, I'm gonna call Eve on three-way."

"No, wait!"

It was too late. The line was already beeping. After a moment, Eve's husky voice sounded in her ear. "What's up, witches?"

"I was telling Tina that I was thinking of her," Lacey said. "It's her birthday tomorrow."

"Oh yeah! We should do something," Eve said. "It's gonna be a full moon. Wanna go hang out in the cemetery? We can do gravestone rubbings and, like, cast spells or some shit."

"No thanks. Cemeteries creep me out," Tina said, twirling the turquoise phone cord around her finger. "I do want to hang out with you guys, though."

"What about the skating rink? We haven't gone together in, like, a bajillion years," Lacey said. "My softball team goes every Friday and we have a blast."

Tina flinched. Hanging out with Lacey's new softball friends was not her idea of birthday fun. "I was kind of thinking we could do something else with just the three of us. Like the old days. It's dumb, but my mom suggested a sleepover."

"Perfect!" Eve said. "We can rent movies and stuff."

"I'll bring snacks!" Lacey chimed in.

Tina's cheeks flushed as a smile crept across her lips. Maybe she had been wrong about her best friends after all. Maybe they hadn't forgotten about her and the promises they made to each other all those years ago.

Best friends. Forever.

"Okay, cool. See you guys this Saturday then?"

"For sure," Lacey said.

"Bad ass." Eve yawned. "Later, witches."

The line went dead and Tina returned the clear handset to the receiver. Maybe a sleepover would be fun after all. Or maybe it would be a disaster, like in the fifth grade when they dared each other to eat a bunch of Mentos and soda at the same time. Her mom had to rent a carpet cleaner after Lacey barfed her guts up everywhere. Either way, it was too late now. A slumber party birthday it was going to be.

Tina washed her face, brushed her teeth and picked out what she wanted to wear for the day. She dressed in a pair of pink floral Bongo shorts with a matching t-shirt, pulled her hair into a scrunchie and spritzed herself all over with Raspberry Sparkle body spray. The soft thud of the front door closing told Tina that her mother had left for work for the day, meaning she had the house all to herself. Another long, lonely summer day stretched out in front of her, spent alone with nothing to do but paint her nails and watch talk shows and reruns. Maybe later she would ride her bike to the library or play Super Mario. But at that moment, she had another important task to attend to; one that caused her stomach to clench and her heart to squeeze in her chest.

She walked to the hallway closet, grabbed a flashlight and gazed up at the pull-down attic door. Tina wasn't looking forward to what she needed to do, but there was something in that attic that she knew would make her slumber party a hit. When they had redecorated her room last year, Tina stored what was left of her stuff in the attic — sentimental toys she couldn't quite yet part with. Stuffed animals. Paperback books. Barbie dolls. The things from her childhood that still held a special place in her heart, including her favorite board game.

Tina held her breath and pulled the cord to the attic door. The door swung open with a creak and dust fluttered into her eyes as she pulled down the folded ladder. She flipped on the flashlight and ascended the stairs, the farty sulfurous flavor of eggs gurgling in her throat. Tina hated the attic and its exposed beams, dusty surfaces, and dark, creepy corners.

She reached the top rung of the ladder and shined the beam of light to where her box of toys was located. A pair of eyes flashed at her in the dark and she let out a yelp. Her heart beat fast and she let out a nervous giggle as their Santa Claus yard decoration smiled at her with bright, rosy cheeks.

"Take a chill pill, T," she said to herself. "It's only a dusty old attic."

Tina grabbed the cardboard box, opened the lid and her hand closed around a rectangular frame. She pulled the object out and her heart squeezed. A framed photograph of Lacey, Eve and herself from their first sleepover smiled back at her, each of the girls donning side ponytails and missing teeth. They had made puff paint t-shirts that year that said "BFF" when they stood side-by-side. Tina was the "B" and Lacey and Eve were both "F's". Were they still BFF's? Her birthday party sleepover would surely tell.

She wedged the photo under her arm and dug into the box again, her hand closing around the item she came for; a rectangular box. A board game, in fact. She pulled the box out and shined the flashlight on the lid. The word OUIJA illuminated ominously in the light of her flashlight. She ran a hand over the words, re-membering the shrieks of laughter that the spirit board brought her and her best friends during so many slum-ber party nights.

BANG!

Tina screamed and shined her flashlight toward the

source of the startling noise. Again two eyes shone at her in the light, this time accompanied by a low hissing sound. An opossum stared back at her, still as can be, its mouth gaping open and displaying rows of little pointy, white teeth. Tina tucked the Ouija board under her arm and flew down the ladder as fast as her feet could take her. She made a mental note to tell her mother about the opossum as she folded up the ladder and closed the attic door. That was enough attic time for today.

Dusty and hopped up on adrenaline, Tina flew to her room and slammed the door behind her. She placed the framed photo on her dresser and sat the Ouija board next to it, still shaken up by the encounter with the opossum. She scowled at her dust-covered reflection in the mirror over the dresser and wiped a bead of sweat from her brow. In two days, she would be sixteen, and Monday marked the first day of 10th grade. After this weekend, she knew everything would change, hopefully for the better. Tina closed her eyes and made a wish. She wanted everything to be the way it used to be — her and Lacey and Eve. Best Friends Forever.

If only she knew just how long forever could be.

Chapter Two

"**W**hat kind of ice cream do you want, sweetie? Chocolate or vanilla?"

Tina shivered as she joined her mother in the freezer section at Publix that following day. Grocery stores always felt extra cold in the summertime, but standing next to the wall of ice cream, the chill seeped all the way through to her bones. She poked her finger on the door and traced a heart shape into the frosted glass.

"Neapolitan," Tina said, rubbing the gooseflesh from her arms. "Strawberry for me, chocolate for Lacey, and vanilla for Eve. One flavor for each of us."

"That's right. I'm so glad the girls are coming over tonight."

"Me too," she said. "Thanks for the idea."

"I'm sorry I didn't get you a present yet," her mother said. "If you want, we can go to the mall and get some Glamour Shots done."

Tina shuddered, remembering the last time they had professional photos taken at the mall. She was eight, her parents had just gotten divorced and her mother wanted to get some sultry photos for the dating service ads. Back then, her mother had a string of boyfriends, but nowadays she seemed to fill her time with binge shopping and sleeping pills instead. Tina wasn't sure which was worse. Back then in her mother's early single days, Tina begrudgingly went with her to get Glamour Shots and ended up dressed in some bright pink and black lace cowgirl ensemble. It wasn't that she didn't like dressing up or putting on makeup, but with her stubborn acne and a body she didn't feel comfortable in, getting "glamorous" was the last thing on her mind.

"No thanks," she said. "I would like a new boom box, though. Purple. And a subscription to the CD of the Month Club."

"You got it, kiddo," her mother said. "Okay, so we just need to pick up your cake, some diet soda, and a couple of frozen pizzas. Do we need anything else?"

Tina shook her head. "Eve is going to drive us to the video store to rent some tapes. Lacey said she was bringing snacks."

"Speak of the devil. Isn't that Lacey over by the magazines?"

Tina turned to the front of the grocery store, and sure enough, there she was. Lacey Dennison's short blonde hair was pulled up into a sporty ponytail, a smile set on her pink lips as she flipped through the latest edition of *Seventeen Magazine*. Her arms were toned and tanned against her white tank top, likely from being outdoors with her softball team all spring and summer. She glowed like an angel, her body surrounded by a soft halo under the fluorescent overhead lights.

Tina walked over to her, absent-mindedly snapping her scrunchie against her wrist. "Hey, Lace."

"Tiny!" She turned to greet her, an exuberant smile spread across her lips. Tina hated the childhood nickname, but always gave Lacey a pass. The two friends embraced in a warm hug, and for a brief moment, the entire world seemed to melt away. Tina couldn't remember the last time they had seen each other. The last day of school? At that moment it didn't matter. Lacey's arms blazed hot as the sun against her chilled skin, warming her from the outside in. Tina breathed in her cinnamon scent and feel-good chemicals rushed through her veins.

"Happy birthday!" Lacey said. "What are you doing here?"

"Mom and I are grabbing stuff for the party tonight," she said.

"Me too, I was picking up some magazines and Cool Ranch Doritos and then I was going to head over to your place." She bit her lower lip, her gaze trailing up and down her form. "So, how does it feel to be sixteen?"

Tina shrugged. "The same as it did to be fifteen, I guess."

"Are you going to get your driver's license?"

"Yeah, probably next week," she lied. The truth was, Tina had failed her drivers' exam. Twice. Driving was scary, and she didn't like being behind the wheel.

"It's so cool to have your own independence, you know?" Lacey snapped her bubble gum. "I mean, even though I have to drive my mom's minivan, it's still cool. We weren't lucky enough to get a new Dodge Neon on our sweet sixteen like Eve. I'm sure you'll get a car eventually though, right?"

"I guess." Tina glanced over her shoulder. Her

mother was already in the checkout line. "I gotta help my mom. I'll see you back at my house?"

"Definitely. Can't wait!"

"Bye."

Tina waited as her mother paid for the groceries and nervously glanced back toward the magazine rack. Lacey had already left, and part of Tina wished she had gone with her. She didn't think Lacey or Eve or anyone wanted to be around her, but maybe she was just insecure. Maybe her friends did still care about their history and friendship. Either way, this sleepover birthday party had to be perfect, or Tina was certain she would lose them for good.

As they walked out of the grocery store, a wave of hot, dry wind hit her like a wall. The gust blew around her in a tornado of heat, a hair dryer set to full blast. Tina caught a glimpse of her reflection in the mirrored windows as her too-long bangs fluttered in her eyes. She cocked her head to the side and squinted as something dark and fuzzy hovered over her shoulder. She paused, staring at her reflection as the dark, fuzzy blob shifted and solidified into the shape of man.

"Get away from me!" Tina whipped around with her hands held high and curled into fists. She swung into nothing but air.

"Tina!" Her mother threw her a puzzled look. "Come on. The ice cream is melting."

Tina let out a shuddered breath, her heartbeat glugging in her ears as she scanned the parking lot. No sign of the thing she had seen, only puzzled shoppers pushing overloaded grocery carts. She glanced back at her reflection to make sure, but the black, fuzzy blob was gone.

"Did your Dad call you yet?"

Tina finished putting away the last of the birthday party groceries as her mother sorted through the mail later that afternoon. She squished the carton of neapolitan ice cream between her fingers and frowned. The ice cream had indeed melted halfway like her mother said it would. Hopefully, it would stiffen up again by the time her friends got there.

"No. He's on a business trip. Japan this time, I think," Tina said. "He'll call and wish me a happy birthday when he gets back."

"Sure he will." Her mom let out a doubtful snort. "One of those fashion catalogs you like came in the mail today. Maybe you can guilt him into buying you some back-to-school clothes."

"Already planned on it." Tina grabbed the dARiA*s magazine from her mother's grip. An exuberant girl with jet black bangs wearing a plaid mini skirt and over-sized sweater winked back at her. The tagline "ToO kEwL 4 sKeWl" was emblazoned across her chest, along with other spoiler blurbs advertising the fall fashion treasures that would surely be inside. Tina loved highlighting all of the rings and shoes and handbags and gleaning fashion inspiration from within the glossy pages.

"What's the plan for tonight then?"

Tina opened up a bag of baby carrots and examined one. "Eve is going to drive us to the video rental place. Then when we come back, we'll probably do manicures and watch movies and eat snacks and stuff."

"Sounds good. No sneaking out though!" Her mother wagged a finger at her, a playful smirk set on her lips. "Just because Eve has a car doesn't mean you can drive around late at night."

"*Mom*," Tina whined. "We won't."

"I'll make pancakes in the morning," she said. "With sprinkles, the way you all like them."

"Sure." Tina turned and rolled her eyes. Even though she was turning sixteen, she suspected her mom still thought they were twelve.

"Remember when you all used grandpa's camcorder to make music videos?" Her mother sighed. "Was it *New Kids on the Block* you all danced to? I can't remember. Ah, you girls have grown up too fast."

"Don't remind me." Tina groaned and bit into the baby carrot. She made a face and spit out the bite of food. "Ew!"

"What's wrong?"

Tina held up the other end of the baby carrot to see what she had bitten into. What looked like a fat, black worm squiggled in the center of the orange carrot. Or at least, half of it did.

"Gross! I think I ate a worm!"

Tina's stomach turned at the revelation. She gagged and ran to the sink, coughing and hacking up the remnants of chewed carrot and severed worm.

"I just bought those! I'm calling the produce manager about this," her mother said, examining the carrot bag. "I expect better from Publix."

Tina rinsed her mouth with water as the doorbell rang. The flavor of mashed worm and carrot still lingered on her tongue as she raced to the front door. A brand new black Dodge Neon was parked in the driveway, its dark, glossy paint job shining in the late afternoon sunlight. Her friends had arrived. Tina held her breath as her hand closed over the front door knob.

Everything is cool, she told herself. *This is going to be the best birthday party sleepover ever.*

Chapter Three

E ve floated into the living room in a wave of black lace and heady gardenia scented perfume. Her long, formerly brown hair had been dyed pitch black, and her eyes, lips and nails were painted a deep hue to match. Evangeline Narvaez was the niece of the head pastor at the Iglesia Cristiana downtown, and Tina guessed that her new interests and fashion choices weren't exactly going over well at home. Even though she wasn't into the whole goth look, Tina still appreciated her friend's bravery for being her authentic self.

"What's your damage?" Eve flopped on the couch and gave Tina a look of disapproval.

"What do you mean?"

"You look like Jeremy Richards when he got pantsed on the last day of school." Eve inspected her manicure. "Seriously, you look upset. What's up?"

"Oh, I bit into a gross carrot before you came over. It's nothing," Tina wiped her mouth. "Anyway, thanks for coming over."

"Yeah, it's gonna be fun," Eve said. "When Lacey gets here we can hit the road and grab some movies."

"Great. I actually ran into her at the grocery store earlier."

"Have you told her yet?" Eve whispered, her dark lips set into a smirk.

Heat rose to Tina's cheeks. Back at Eve's birthday party at the end of the school year, Tina had too much sugar and spilled a long-held secret to her friend. It was a secret she meant to keep, but Eve managed to get it out of her in a moment of weakness.

"No. I don't think I can."

"It's the perfect timing! It's your birthday, she has to be nice about it," Eve said. "Besides, do you wanna die never having confessed to your crush?"

"Who has a crush?" Tina's mother waltzed into the living room with wide eyes. "Evangeline! I almost didn't recognize you!"

"Hey Ms. Martin," Eve said. "We were talking about this cute guy at the video store, Deon. I have a huge crush on him."

"All the more reason to go rent video tapes then." Her mother winked. "I'm gonna go grab a shower and get out of your hair. You girls have fun."

"Thanks, Mom." Tina flashed Eve a death stare.

When she was certain her mother was out of ear shot, Tina joined her friend on the couch. "I'm not going to say anything tonight or probably ever. Please don't bring it up again."

"Okay, okay." Eve giggled. "I'm just trying to be a good wing woman."

"Gee, *thanks*."

Eve leaned over and gave her a hug. "Happy b-day, T. This is gonna be fun."

The doorbell rang and Tina jumped up to answer it. Lacey had arrived. She flung the door open and was met with a deafening squeal.

"Happy birthday! Eeeee!"

Lacey stood in the doorway grinning from ear-to-ear, with a bouquet of balloons in one hand and a wrapped present in the other. She jumped up and down and the balloons bounced with her, making an echoey, sproinging plastic sound.

"Oh, my GOD! How did you get so many balloons?"

"Sixteen, in fact." Lacey handed her the balloon bouquet. "I remembered how much you liked balloons."

"Thanks, Lace." Tina said. "Let me drop these off in my room and we can head out to get some tapes."

Tina deposited the balloons in her bedroom, grabbed her mini backpack purse, and returned to the living room. Lacey and Eve were whispering and turned to face her when Tina reappeared. Her heart dropped to her feet as their serious expressions turned to smiles. Had they been whispering about her?

Tina cleared her throat and crossed her arms in front of her. "What were you guys talking about?"

"I was telling Lacey about Deon," Eve said. "He's so rad. I bet he'll let us use his employee discount."

"Oh. Cool." Tina exhaled and hitched her purse over her shoulder. "Let's hit it."

Tina shuddered in the passenger seat of Eve's car as a

cool breeze blasted from the air conditioner. The pristine Dodge Neon still had that new car scent paired with Eve's witchy perfume. A woman on the radio sang about drinking blood in New Orleans and Eve sang along with the lyrics.

Finally, they reached the shopping plaza where the video rental store was located. Eve parked and the three friends linked arms and strolled up to the entrance.

"Welcome to Cool Flix." The boy behind the counter greeted them and winked, his gaze locked onto Eve. His eyebrow ring and black nail polish seemed out of place against the buttoned up blue work shirt, but somehow, he pulled off the look.

"Hey, Deon." Eve purred and cozied up to the counter. "Got any good new releases?"

"*12 Monkeys* just came out," he said. "I think we might have one left on the shelf."

"Hmm, I don't like Brad Pitt," Eve said. "He's too pretty."

"I dunno, he looked kinda gross in the previews," Lacey said. "I'm gonna go check out the comedy section."

"I'll go with you." Tina gave Eve one last glance as she leaned over the counter and giggled. She was happy for her friend, but a small pang of jealousy wiggled its way into her heart. Tina wanted that same thing that Eve had with Deon for herself. The possibility of connection, the pining, the desire. Someone to hold hands with. Someone to love. It was hard to be happy for her friend when she only felt disappointment and despair.

Tina wandered over to the horror section as Lacey perused the comedies. She approached a tape with a cover she had never seen before. The artwork was simple, but creepy and eye-catching; a single bright pink pentagram against a black background. There was no title or credits, no information of any kind. Tina reached for it as Lacey squealed her name.

"Tina, look! They have *Clueless*!" She said, holding up the plastic VHS case. "I love Alicia Silverstone."

Tina turned and shook her head. "We've seen it a bunch of times. How about *Empire Records*?"

Tina sensed a strange pressure over her shoulder. The hairs on the back of her neck stood at attention. A pit of anxiety welled up in her gut. Something, or someone, was behind her.

"Boo!" Eve poked her in the side. "I thought we were renting scary movies?"

"Oh my gawd, Eve," Tina said. "You scared me half

to death."

"So jumpy," Eve smirked and grabbed a tape from the display. "We should rent *Candyman*. I love a handsome, vengeful ghost."

"You only like Candyman because he looks like Deon." Lacy smiled and glanced toward the front of the video store.

"Damn straight," Eve said. "Maybe if we're lucky we can call him tonight."

"Deon?" Tina said.

"No! I mean Candyman." Eve rolled her eyes. "Seriously. *Candyman* or *Pumpkinhead*. Which one?"

Eve held up both clamshell boxes. Tina had always been equally terrified and fascinated with the cover art on horror movie VHS covers as a little kid. She loved being scared, but also feared so many real world things at the same time. Watching scary movies with her friends was the best, like riding a rollercoaster. They could grip each other tightly and scream together, experiencing the thrills and chills from the safety of home.

"Let's just get all of them," Tina said. "We can watch *Clueless* afterwards if we're totally freaked out."

"Perfect." Eve grabbed all the tapes and headed toward the checkout desk.

"Let's give the love birds a minute alone." Lacey whispered and grabbed Tina's hand.

The two friends waited outside as Eve flirted with Deon. Tina leaned against her car, the black exterior warm and comforting against her skin.

"Hey," Lacey said. "I'm glad we're doing this."

"Yeah, me too."

"I'm sorry if it seems like I've been a little distant lately. I know we don't spend as much time together as we used to."

"That's okay." Tina sighed. "Things change, people change and all that."

"We haven't changed though," Lacey said. "You're always going to be my best friend. No matter what."

"Thanks, Lace. You're always going to be my best friend, too."

Tina glanced up at the glass front door of the video store at her and Lacey's mirrored reflection. Her body froze as she realized that the black blob had returned. The dark mass hovered over Tina's right shoulder, a billowing smoke cloud reflected in the afternoon sunlight. Her limbs tingled and her throat tightened as she watched the blob take the shape of a man once more.

"Lacey," Tina said, her voice squeaking. "Do you see that?"

"See what?"

"In the window. The figure next to me. Do you see it?"

"No, I ..."

"Let's go, witches!" Eve held the tapes high as she burst out the door.

Tina's pulse sped up and the flavor of pennies filled her mouth. She held her breath, anticipating that something awful would happen as her limbs remained locked in fear. She stared at the front of the video store, watching and waiting as the glass front door closed. She let out a sigh of relief. The dark mass was gone.

"Hello! Birthday girl? Earth to Tina!" Lacey waved her hand in front of Tina's face. "Let's go!"

"Sorry." Tina exhaled and shook her head. "I thought I saw something."

Chapter Four

"*Happy birthday dear Tina, happy birthday to you!*"

Tina gazed up at the expectant faces of her mother and best friends over the glow of sixteen candles. The birthday cake her mother had picked out for her read "Happy Birthday Tina, Sweet Sixteen" and was framed with a bouquet of pink frosting rosettes. She closed her eyes, made a silent, secret wish, and blew. Everyone clapped as Eve turned on the dining room light.

"Who wants a piece of cake?" Tina's mother held up an oversized kitchen knife.

"Not me. I'm stuffed," Eve said. "Too much pizza."

"I'll have some," Lacey said. "Just a small slice."

"Me too," Tina said.

"Open your presents!" Lacey shoved a giant box across the table.

"Aw, you really didn't have to get me anything." Tina slid her finger underneath the pink striped wrapping paper. A sharp, hot burst of pain shot through her finger as she separated the paper from the package. She jerked her hand back as a thin line of red bloomed on her fingertip. "Ow!"

Tina stuck her finger in her mouth and tasted acid. She glanced across the table to the big picture window where four smiling figures reflected back.

No—Five.

Tina froze again as the dark figure hovered over her right shoulder in the window reflection.

"Is ... Is anyone else seeing this?" She asked and pointed to the reflection.

Lacey glanced at the window. "See what?"

"Do you all see something behind me?" Tina asked, her voice high and shaky. She turned to look over her right shoulder, and, like before, nothing was there. When she looked back, there were only four figures in the window reflection.

"Tina? Baby?" Her mom put a hand on her shoulder. "You okay?"

Tina shook her head and forced a smile.

"I'm fine. Nevermind."

She returned to her gift and tried to brush off what she had seen. Maybe she just needed to go to the eye doctor again? Or maybe she was getting migraines like Gina Folkerson did when they were in the 7th grade. Or maybe she was losing her mind. Either way, whatever was going on would have to wait until after her sleep-over. Nothing was going to get in the way of this one special night with her friends.

Tina lifted the lid of the box inside and gasped.

"No way!" The shirt inside was old and faded, but it was one she knew well. "Lacey! You don't have to give me this!"

"I know how much you always wanted a *No Fear* shirt of your own," she said. "I couldn't find one in your size at the store. I don't wear it anymore, so I figured I would pass it on to you."

Tina held the black t-shirt to her nose and inhaled. Cinnamon. It even smelled like Lacey. She gazed down at the soft cotton tee as a pair of menacing eyes stared back at her under the signature *No Fear* label. This would be her new favorite sleep shirt.

"That's not all. Look in the box!" Lacey clapped.

Tina reached into the box and pulled out a CD. A boy wearing a cape against a yellow background gazed back at her.

"I know you don't really listen to rap, but these guys are good!" Lacey said. "It's kinda like rock and rap?"

"Cool," Tina said, heat rushing to her cheeks. "This is awesome. Thank you."

"Here, open mine." Eve held out a small square box wrapped in black shiny paper. "I got it at the mall."

"Thanks." Tina opened up the package more carefully this time with her still throbbing fingertip. She lifted the lid of the box and her eyes widened. Inside was a y-shaped necklace inlaid with blood red jewels on a pewter and black chain. "Eve! This is amazing! How did you know I wanted one of these?"

"I saw you circled them in the winter dARiA*s magazine," Eve said with a smirk. "I figured you could use a little touch of goth in your wardrobe."

"I love it."

Tina's chest swelled with love for her friends. They did still care about her. "Thanks. This means a lot to me."

"Well, girls, I'm gonna put this cake away and head

to bed," her mother said. She leaned in and gave Tina a peck on the cheek. "You all have fun tonight. Knock if you need anything."

"Thanks, Ms. Martin." Eve waved and offered an innocent-looking smile.

"Yeah, thank you," Lacey said.

"G'night, Mom."

Tina and her friends waited until the lock on her mother's door made an audible "click". They smiled at each other and rose from the table sporting matching mischievous grins.

"All right, witches," Eve said. "Let's get this party started!"

"Don't you think your mom will be mad when she sees this?" Lacey stood in the doorway of Tina's en suite bathroom, her teeth set in a grimace.

Eve held a sewing needle in one hand and an ink pen in the other. "It's going to be on her hip. She won't see it."

"Are you sure this will work?" Tina laid back on her

bathroom floor and stared up at the ceiling. She was wearing the *No Fear* shirt that Lacey had given her, the hem tucked into her jean shorts with cuffs rolled at the sleeve. At that moment, she wished that she didn't have any fear, but her stomach was turning somersaults at the thought of needles and blood.

"You're not afraid of needles, are you?" Eve asked.

"No," Tina lied.

"Good, because you're going to have to tattoo me next." Eve flicked on the lighter and burned the sharp end of the needle.

"Have you ever done this before?" Lacey asked.

"No, but I saw my brother do it a bunch of times," Eve said. "Okay, T. Get ready."

Tina closed her eyes and held her breath. It was after 11 p.m. and they had already burned through most of their sleepover activities. The snacks were all consumed. They had already watched one of the VHS tapes, witnessing as Pumpkinhead sought his revenge on a group of careless teens. They even gave each other scratchy peach exfoliation facials and manicures. Eve suggested sneaking out to go to the cemetery. Lacey suggested they make prank calls to some boys from school. Tina didn't want to do either of those things, so matching poke and stick BFF tattoos it would have to be.

Before Eve could land the first mark on her skin, Tina's finger pulsed. Red glazed across her vision as the dark figure wormed its way into her thoughts again. Suddenly, she felt sick to her stomach.

"Wait!" Tina sat up from her position on the floor and crawled to the toilet. A gush of birthday cake, Cool Ranch Doritos, soda, and frozen pizza flowed from her guts in a hot wave. Lacey rushed to her side and held her hair back as Tina heaved the last of her birthday party treats into the bowl.

"Ugh. Gross." She wiped the back of her mouth and flushed the toilet. "I need to brush my teeth."

"Okay, so no DIY tattoos," Eve sighed. "Message received."

"Sorry. I don't know what's wrong with me," Tina said, rinsing her mouth out at the sink. She blobbed a pearl of toothpaste on her toothbrush and ran it through her teeth. She didn't want to look up at her reflection in the mirror as she brushed for fear of what she might see.

"What's up with you, T?" Lacey asked. "You've been off all day. Are you sick? We can go home and do this another time ..."

"No!" Tina shouted. "Sorry, I mean, I know I haven't been acting like myself. I've been seeing some weird stuff lately. I probably need to get my eyes checked."

"Bad stuff? Like what?" Eve asked.

Tina hesitated. These were her best friends. If she couldn't tell them, who could she tell?

"All day, I've been seeing this weird dark mass hovering over my right shoulder," she said. "I only see it in the reflection of windows or mirrors. It turns into the shape of a man and then disappears."

"That's creepy as hell," Lacey said.

"I've got just the thing." Eve got up off the floor and walked into the bedroom. She picked the Ouija board up off Tina's dresser and held it out toward her two friends. "Let's see if we can talk to whatever is haunting you."

Tina's anxiety spiked. At that moment, the graveyard or a tattoo sounded like a better option. "I don't know. I pulled the game out of the attic because I thought it might be fun. Now, I'm not so sure."

"Oh, come on! We used to love playing with the Ouija board," Lacey said. "Remember that time we asked where your mom's lost diamond earring was?"

"Yeah. The spirit board said to look in the back-yard next to Mom's potting bench," Tina said. "It was right."

"Well, whaddaya think?" Lacey asked, joining Eve on her bed.

Eve had already unboxed the board and the triangular planchette. "Please?"

Tina nodded and let out a sigh. "Okay. But only for a minute."

Chapter Five

Tina's room was dark, save for the soft glow of two lavender scented candles she had picked up on sale at the mall. She had a bad feeling about this— about what they were going to do. As kids, telling ghost stories and playing with the Ouija board had been fun. They liked scaring each other and didn't take any of their mystical games seriously. But after the strange things going on leading up to her birthday, Tina had little interest in connecting with the dead.

As usual, Eve took the reins and led the board game seance. Even when they were small, she always had the most interest in spooky stuff out of the three friends. Eve was always trying to get them to make wishes, cast spells or practice their psychic and telekinetic abilities to no results. In hindsight, it really wasn't that surprising that her stylistic tastes turned to the dark side as well. For Tina, it had been all fun, but for Eve, communing with the spirit world was serious business.

"Oh, magical Ouija board. Hear our words! Are there any spirits in this houuuuuse?" Eve sat erect on the bed, her eyes closed and her chin tipped upward with both of her pointer and index fingers gently touching the planchette. Lacey mirrored Eve's position, giving Tina a conspiratorial side-eye as they sat in silence and waited for something to happen. Tina hugged her pillow and peered at them from the far end of the bed as her two best friends attempted to summon something from the other side.

"Oh, spirits," Eve called out in a dreamy voice. "Can you hear meeeee?"

"A little heavy-handed, dontcha think?" Lacey snorted.

"I'm just trying to set the mood."

"Well, it's not working. We've been sitting here for almost five minutes and nothing has happened," Lacey said. "Besides, it only works if we are all touching the thingy. Come on, Tina. We need you, too."

Lacey waved for Tina to join them and placed her fingers gently on the planchette. Tina paused again, unsure if she really wanted to take part. She didn't actually believe in ghosts or metaphysical stuff; the Ouija board was nothing more than a toy they used to mess around with at sleepovers. But after the strange occurrences that had happened that day, she wasn't so sure what she believed anymore. If she just stayed on the sidelines, she might never know if what she had seen and experienced was real.

"Okay." Tina tossed her pillow behind her and joined her friends at the spirit board. She placed her fingertips on the planchette, expecting to feel a jolt of electricity rush through her. She relaxed a little when nothing happened. It was only a child's toy after all.

"Let me try this time," Lacey said and cleared her throat. "Oh, spirits or whatever. Does anyone have a crush on me?"

The candles flickered and the planchette trembled under their fingertips.

Eve squealed and broke away from the board. "Who did that?"

"Not me!" Lacey said.

"Me neither," Tina said. "It was moving on its own."

"I told you it needed all three of us!" Lacey said. "Eve, put your fingers back. I wanna know who has a crush on me."

"Maybe this isn't such a good idea," Tina said. "Let's make some prank calls instead."

"After! Let's do this now!" Lacey grabbed Tina's hands and plopped them back on the board. "Concentrate."

"Fine." Tina cringed.

Lacey closed her eyes again and breathed in deeply. "Spirits. Is someone out there thinking about me?"

The planchette jerked back to life under their combined touch. Horrified, Tina watched as the clear glass indicator crept across the board and paused.

"T!" Lacey exclaimed. "Oh, I hope it's Tommy Myers. He borrowed my pencil on the last day of school and never gave it back."

"I don't think it's Tommy," Eve said, flicking her gaze to Tina. "Besides, he wears the same dirty socks for days. Gross."

"Quiet!" Lacey hissed. "Let's see where it goes next."

The planchette continued its onward creep across the board. Sparkles of adrenaline rushed through Tina's veins as she instinctively knew where the indicator would land next. She was an unwilling participant in her own soon-to-be demise. Her stomach dropped as the glass indicator rested over the letter "I".

"I!" Lacey said. "Oh gawd, I hope it's not Tim Gerlihy. He wears way too much CK One cologne."

"I thought you liked CK One?" Tina glanced at the half-empty bottle on her dresser.

"Yeah, but, he practically takes a bath in it," Lacey said. "Okay, concentrate."

The planchette moved again and sweat beaded on Tina's upper lip. Her heart filled with horror as the triangular object edged ever closer to the letter "N". Her secret was going to be exposed by a stupid kids board game if she didn't do something. Lacey would never speak to her again if the Ouija board spelled out her name, revealing her long-kept secret. She panicked and pressed down on the planchette, sending it shooting off the bed and onto the floor.

"Eeeee!"

Lacey screamed. Eve jumped off the bed and bumped into Tina's dresser, sending all of the contents on top sailing. Her Caboodle exploded on the floor, scattering makeup brushes, mascaras, hair ties, and a rainbow of *Wet & Wild* nail polish and lip glosses.

The framed photo of the three friends when they were younger flew, and for a moment, Tina almost imagined that it was suspended in midair. Gravity finally claimed the picture of the trio of smiling eight-year-olds and sent it crashing to the floor, cracking the glass in two.

"Oh crap! Tina, I'm so sorry." Eve picked up the broken picture frame and handed it to her. "Our picture. I ruined it."

"It's okay. I can get another frame," Tina said. "Maybe the Ouija board isn't such a good idea though."

"I'll help clean this stuff up," Lacey said, scooping up the contents of the Caboodle. "Ooh. Dr. Pepper flavored lip gloss."

THUNK.

"What was that?" Lacey whispered.

The three friends glanced up at the ceiling and held their breath.

THUNK. THUNK. THUNK.

"Crap," Tina said. "I forgot to tell my mom about the opossum."

"What opossum?" Eve asked.

"I saw one in the attic earlier when I went to dig out the Ouija board," Tina said. "Scared me half to death."

"Oh, I wanna see!" Lacey said. "I love opossums."

"Remember when we used to go up in the attic and dress up in all of your mom's weird old clothes?" Eve walked to the door. "I'm bored. Let's go see what's up there."

"It's just gross and dusty up there," Tina said.

"C'mon," Lacey said, taking her hand. "It'll be fun."

"Fine."

The Ouija board was forgotten as Tina grabbed her flashlight. She crept down the dark hall behind her friends toward the pull-down ladder. Even though she wasn't looking forward to going back up into the attic, she was grateful to the opossum for the distraction. She glanced over her shoulder at the master bedroom on the other side of the house to check if the coast was clear. A flashing light blipped in the dark, a thin blue line of television fuzz under her mother's bedroom door. Her mother was likely already heavily medicated and so deep in dreamland that she wouldn't hear them.

Lacey reached up and slowly pulled the cord to the fold-down ladder. Despite her best attempts, the hinges on the old wooden door still creaked.

"Shhh!" Tina handed Lacey the flashlight.

"Don't worry so much," Eve said. "Your mom never wakes up. She takes the same sleeping pills my mom does."

"It's not my mom I'm worried about," Tina said.

Lacey ascended the ladder and Eve followed behind. The attic was the last place Tina wanted to go to, but she didn't want to disappoint her friends either. A thrill danced down her spine as she remembered the dark form in the reflection of the windows and the feeling that she was being watched. She sensed it again as her friends disappeared into the attic — a pressure at her back, something heavy looming over her shoulder. Whispering in her ear.

Let me out.

Let me in.

No. Tina wasn't going to give into her intrusive thoughts. She had let her anxiety get the best of her far too many times, but not tonight. Tonight she was going to enjoy these last few moments of childhood with her BFF's.

"Suck it up, buttercup." Tina blew her bangs out of her eyes in a frustrated huff and followed her friends up the ladder into the dark attic. But before she reached the top rung, Lacey let out a high-pitched scream.

"Oh my gawd!"

Something clattered and fell to the attic floor with

a loud *THUNK*. Tina's blood chilled as she forced her frozen legs to climb to the top of the ladder.

Her friends were in trouble, and she needed to get to them *now*.

Chapter Six

"So this is where your Barbie collection went!"

Lacey held a disheveled doll in her hand and shined the flashlight on its plastic face. Blonde strands of hair stuck out at wild angles from the dolls' head thanks to a DIY haircut Tina gave her years ago. The once adorable feminine figure was half dressed and her legs were covered in Crayola marker tattoos that bled in fuzzy lines against her sticky, rubbery skin.

Tina gasped and collapsed in a heap, feeling as rough as her former fashion doll looked. "Lacey! You scared the life outta me! I thought you were hurt!"

"The only thing hurt is my feelings," Eve said, holding up a plush Garfield stuffed animal. "Didn't I get you this for your tenth birthday?"

"Yeah. I still like Garfield," Tina said.

"Why is all of this stuff up here?" Lacey asked.

"I couldn't bring myself to give this stuff away yet." Tina dug into her toy box and picked up Rainbow Dash, her favorite My Little Pony. Her thoughts drifted back to simpler times when the contents of the toy box were her prized treasures. A time when she didn't doubt Lacey and Eve's friendship. A time when things were easier, more lighthearted and fun. Maybe that's the real reason her toys were hidden away in a dusty attic. She knew that time was long gone. It was easier to move on without the evidence of better days always smacking her in the face.

"No biggie. It's just kids stuff." Eve unceremoniously tossed the plush Garfield back into the box. "So where is this opossum anyway?"

Tina shrugged. "It was over in the corner the other day. It kind of hissed at me and then froze up."

"I heard they play dead," Lacey said.

"They're so ugly," Eve said, pulling a disgusted face.

"I think they're cute." Lacey shined the light in the corner of the attic. "Well, it's not there now."

"See?" Tina said. "Nothing to see up here. Let's go."

"Hold on. What's this?" Lacey pulled out a scrapbook and began flipping through the pages. "Is this us?"

"Yeah." Tina's cheeks heated as she remembered the contents of the scrapbook. She had spent so many hours cutting out photographs of her and Lacey and Eve and gluing them to the pages. She had saved ticket stubs to movies they went to, birthday party invitations, bubble gum wrappers, secret notes, fortune tellers made from origami and M.A.S.H. games. The entire history of their friendship was pressed between those pages, covered in glitter and neon kitten stickers. Now it was collecting dust in a dark attic along with the rest of her childhood things.

"I get why you put your toys away, but why is this up here?" Lacey gazed over at her, a pained expression on her face.

Tina sighed. "I ... I didn't think you guys were my friends anymore."

"Seriously?" Eve propped a hand on her hip. "Why?"

"I dunno," Tina cupped her hot cheeks. "Lacey has her softball friends. You have your cool goth crowd you hang out with now. I'm just a boring nobody. I guess I feel like I got left behind."

"*Tiny*." Lacey said. "We love you! Don't you know

that?"

"That's why we're here," Eve said, wrapping an arm around her shoulder. "People change, but they don't stop caring about each other."

Tina wiped at her eyes. "I'm sorry, it was stupid of me to think that way."

"I know what you need," Eve said. "Root beer float?"

Tina sniffed and swallowed the lump in her throat. "Yeah. That would be great."

"Good thing I saved some vanilla," Eve said. "Lacey, you gonna have a root beer float?"

"Nah, I'm good. None for *meeeeyeeeee*!!!" Lacey let out a yelp and dropped the flashlight. It clattered to the ground as a low hiss sounded through the air.

"Help!" Lacey said. "No!"

Tina scrambled for the flashlight as the sound of skittering claws scratched on the wooden attic beams. Her hands fumbled along the ground as she searched in the dark, her pulse chugging away like a steam engine.

Nonononono.

Her hand closed around a cylindrical object and Tina allowed a glimmer of hope to enter her heart. She grabbed hold of the end of the flashlight and flicked it on, the light strobing like lightning in the dark. Eve whimpered as Tina shined the beam toward the sound of their screeching friend. A thin, hairless tail flicked in the beam of light and disappeared into the attic void as she illuminated Lacey's red, contorted face.

"It bit me!" Lacey rubbed her wrist and clutched her hand to her chest. "I changed my mind. Opossums *aren't* cute."

"Sorry we were out of vanilla," Eve said, giving Tina an apologetic smile.

Eve sipped her root beer float as the friends Tina's cup remained mostly untouched as they sat on her bed later that evening staring into their root beer floats.

"It's not as good with diet root beer," Lacey mumbled. "The strawberry tastes okay though."

"How's your hand?" Tina asked.

Lacey shrugged and held it up. "Fine. Didn't even leave a mark."

"Sorry you got scared," Tina said. "Are you okay?"

"I'm fine," Lacey said.

"I can't believe your mom didn't wake up." Eve

snorted. "We could probably drop a bomb and she'd sleep right through it."

"Well, it's a good thing," Tina said. "She would have freaked if she knew we were up there. We probably should go to bed soon though."

"Well, I'm not tired yet," Eve said. "What should we do next? Should we try to call Bloody Mary or Candyman in the bathroom?"

"No. Definitely not," Tina said, shuddering at the thought of ghosts trapped in mirrors. "I'm all tapped out on spooky stuff."

"Let's just watch *Clueless*," Lacey yawned. "I'm actually getting kinda tired."

"Lightweight." Tina tossed a pillow at Lacey. "Come on, there's gotta be something else we can do."

"What about, Light as a Feather, Stiff as a Board?" Eve suggested.

"What's that?" Lacey asked.

"Oh, it's super fun," Eve said, digging into her black leather crossbody bag. She pulled out a pocket-sized spiral notebook and flipped it open. "Look, Deon and some of his friends gave me notes on how to do it. You lay on the ground and we each put two fingers underneath your body. Then we recite our names backwards and say *light as a feather, stiff as a board* over and over. Then you *float*."

"That won't work," Lacey said.

"Yes it will!" Eve insisted. "Deon said his friend read the spell in some old book and he hovered, like, three inches off the ground."

"So why don't you do it with Deon?" Tina playfully stuck her tongue out.

"Because the book also said that the spell can only be performed by a coven of three." Eve's gaze flicked back and forth between Lacey and Tina. "Three friends who are bonded."

"Wait, so that really works?" Tina asked.

Eve nodded. "I watched them. It was him and his two best friends. This guy — they called him Rasputin, and some other guy. It was so freaky."

"No way." Tina snorted and crossed her arms at her chest.

"Yes way!" Eve said. "Deon told me that he and his friends did the same thing that we did as kids. That they were bonded—"

"By a promise," Lacey interrupted, her voice flat. "By blood."

"That's right." Eve locked her gaze with Tina. "Remember? Blood sisters?"

Tina's pulse raced as she glanced down at the scar on her palm. They had cut a little too deep into her hand all those years ago. She bled so much that day, but it was worth it. Blood sisters. Best friends forever.

"I guess it doesn't hurt to try," Tina said.

"Yes!" Eve clapped her hands. "Tina, you're the birthday girl. Do you wanna float first?"

"No, I think I'll pass."

"I'll do it." Lacey laid down on Tina's pink carpet.

"Lacey, you don't have to—"

Tina's voice trailed off as a low hum resounded in her ears. She clasped her hands to the side of her head and doubled over as a wave of pain crushed through her. Her brain squeezed inside her skull like the worst migraine imaginable as the hum crescendoed to a whine. And then, as soon as the event began, it was over.

She blinked and gazed at Lacey and Eve, each sporting twin expressions of confusion.

"Uh, Tina." Eve placed a hand on her shoulder. "Are you okay?"

"You guys didn't hear that?"

"Hear what?" Lacey propped herself up on her elbows.

Tina exhaled and shook her head. "I'm losing my mind. Okay. Let's do this."

54

Chapter Seven

E ve got to work right away setting the scene for their game of Light as a Feather, Stiff as a Board. She searched the bedroom and lit every single candle that Tina owned, even the good ones that she had been saving for a special occasion. After all the candles were lit, Eve tucked the lighter into her purse, turned off the lights and positioned herself in a cross-legged stance on the floor next to Lacey's body. Tina sat down across from her and mirrored her stance. All at once, the atmosphere seemed to be still and quiet, as if all of the oxygen had been sucked from the room.

"What do we do first?" Tina asked.

"Lacey is supposed to close her eyes and relax. Lacey!

Close your eyes!" Eve snapped her fingers.

"Okay, okay, sheesh," Lacey said, squeezing her eyes shut. "Better?"

"Yes. Okay, repeat after me," Eve said, reading from a spiral notebook . "Animam meam tibi offero zozo dea perditionis."

"Annie whatie?" Lacey asked.

Eve rolled her eyes. "It's right here. Just read it."

"What does it mean?"

"I dunno, it's magic words that make you float," Eve said. "It's in latin or something. Please try."

"Okay, I'll do my best." Lacey cleared her throat and recited the passage. "Animam meam tibi offero zozo dea perditionis."

A chill rolled down Tina's spine. Like when they were using the Ouija board, something felt off. Her guts twisted, her instincts screaming to tell Lacey not to keep reading. But that wouldn't be very fun of her, would it? All Tina wanted was for her friends to stay. She forced herself to push back on the feelings of dread or else she would spook them away and the party would be over.

"Now I want you to try and relax," Eve said. "According to this, your spirit is supposed to, like, leave your body as we chant and that's how we'll be able to lift you up."

"You didn't say anything about my spirit leaving my body!" Lacey's eyes popped open and she sat up. "What the hell, Eve?"

"It's not for real." Eve rolled her eyes. "Come on."

"Fine." Lacey laid back down and squeezed her eyes shut.

"Then what?" Tina asked.

"Then we both repeat our name backwards and place our fingers gently under her body," Eve said, demonstrating the two-finger touch. "Like this. After that, we chant *light as a feather, stiff as a board* over and over until she's floating."

"How long does it take to work?" Tina asked.

"Only one way to find out," Eve said. "We have to say our full name too, no nicknames. I'll start. Evangeline Narvaez. Zeavran enilegnave!"

"Oh, okay," Tina cleared her throat. "Christina Martin. Nitram anitsirhc!"

Eve wrinkled her nose.

"Did I say it right?" Tina asked.

"I think so."

Eve rubbed her hands and placed her fingers under Lacey's body; two under her shoulder and two under her thigh. Tina mirrored her motions, her paper cut finger snagging on the fabric of Lacey's t-shirt.

"Now we recite the words together over and over until she's off the ground," Eve said, locking eyes with Tina. "Got it?"

Tina nodded. They began the incantation, whispering together in unison.

"Light as a feather, stiff as a board."

"Light as a feather, stiff as a board."

"Light as a feather, stiff as a board."

"Light as a feather, stiff as a board."

"Light as a feather, stiff as a board."

"Light as a feather, stiff as a board."

Lacey's body moved.

Tina gasped.

"No! Keep your focus!" Eve said, her eyes still closed.

"Light as a feather, stiff as a board."

"Light as a feather, stiff as a board."

"Light as a feather, stiff as a board."

"Light as a feather, stiff as a board."

"Light as a feather, stiff as a board."

"Light as a feather, stiff as a board."

Tina's fingers lifted off the floor, and Lacey's body moved with them. Like the incantation stated, she was light as a feather. Filled with helium, just like her sweet sixteen balloons.

"Light as a feather, stiff as a board."

"Light as a feather, stiff as a board."

"Light as a feather, stiff as a board."

"Light as a feather, stiff as a board."

"Light as a feather, stiff as a board."

"Light as a feather, stiff as a board."

Eve and Tina kept their focus as Lacey continued to levitate. Her body truly was light and stiff, her hips level with their eyes now.

"Eve," Tina whispered. "It's working."

"I know!" Eve said. "Stay focused!"

"Light as a feather, stiff as a board."

"Light as a feather, stiff as a board."

"Light as a feather, stiff as a board."

"Light as a feather, stiff as a board."

"Light as a feather, stiff as a board."

"Light as a feather, stiff as a board."

The bouquet of balloons that Lacey brought unraveled, as if released by an unseen hand. They scattered around the room until the tops of their bulbous heads bounced against the ceiling.

"Light as a feather, stiff as a board."

"Light as a feather, stiff as a board."

"Light as a feather, stiff as a board."

"Light as a feather, stiff as a board."

"Light as a feather, stiff as a board."

"Light as a feather, stiff as a board."

"Guys? Is everything okay?" Lacey asked. Her eyes remained closed, her arms draped across her chest in an X. "What's going on?"

"Light as a feather, stiff as a board."

"Light as a feather, stiff as a board."

"Light as a feather, stiff as a board."

"Light as a feather, stiff as a board."

Light as a feather, stiff as a board.

Light as a feather, stiff as a board.

Tina's mouth hung open as Lacey floated higher.

Pop! Pop, pop, pop, pop, pop.

Tina screamed. All sixteen of her birthday balloons burst, as though someone stuck them with a needle.

Lacey's body rushed toward the ceiling.

"Light as a feather, stiff as a board."

"Light as a feather, stiff as a board."

"Light as a feather, stiff as a board."

"Light as a feather, stiff as a board."

"Light as a feather, stiff as a board."

"Light as a feather, stiff as a board."

Tina turned her gaze to Eve. Her friend was still chanting, her hands raised up toward the sky. Eve's dark pupils were gone and Tina could only see the whites of her eyes.

"Light as a feather, stiff as a board."

"Light as a feather, stiff as a board."

"Light as a feather, stiff as a board."

"Light as a feather, stiff as a board."

"Light as a feather, stiff as a board."

"Light as a feather, stiff as a board."

Lacey's face was nearly touching the ceiling. Shards of torn balloon and ribbon floated down to her pink carpet like confetti as Tina clasped her hands to her ears. The pressure in the room shifted, as if they were in an airplane cabin that was descending too fast. This wasn't just some slumber party trick or fun game. This was real, and for the first time, Tina wasn't just afraid, she was genuinely terrified. Like before at the grocery store, a hot blast of hair dryer wind tore through her room, whipping Eve's black hair into a frenzy around her head.

"Light as a feather, stiff as a board."

"Light as a feather, stiff as a board."

"Light as a feather, stiff as a board."

"Light as a feather, stiff as a board."

"Light as a feather, stiff as a board."

"Light as a feather, stiff as a board."

"STOP!" Eve stopped chanting and opened her eyes. Tina curled into a ball and pointed up to the ceiling where their friend remained suspended in midair. Slowly, they both tipped their chins upward toward Lacey's floating body. Eve gasped and her hands flew to her mouth.

"Holy ..."

"How are we going to get her down?" Tina whispered.

"I don't know," Eve said. "I didn't think this would really work."

"Lace?" Tina asked, her voice small and uncertain. "You okay up there?"

A low growl rumbled through the room. Tina and Eve both screamed as the walls shook with the force of a hundred fists pounding the drywall. The windows rattled as though a hurricane raged outside, and the entire room quaked under their feet. Posters fell from the wall, the glass votives from her candles exploded and the drawers of her dresser shook open. And then, as soon as the disturbance happened, it subsided.

Tina glanced up at Lacey and nearly screamed again, but the sound caught in her throat. Her friend's floating body slowly rotated like a chicken on a rotisserie until Lacey was facing them again. Her hair hung in her face, but it didn't obstruct their view of her eyes. Her entire expression was sinister, a sneer set on her bloodless lips, the color drained from her suntanned skin. But it was the eyes that were most terrifying. They *glowed*.

"Lacey?"

Laughter echoed through the room, dark and sinister. Tina and Eve screamed again as their friend's mouth opened to reveal rows of sharp, shiny teeth.

"There is no Lacey," she said, her voice deep and husky. Inhuman. "Only Zozo."

Chapter Eight

W hat in the Ghostbusters hell?"

Eve helped Tina to her feet as their possessed friend floated overhead. They backed up against
the wall as Lacey's body convulsed. "Eve, what do we
do?" Tina clasped her hands over her ears and cursed
herself for not listening to her instincts.

Lacey continued to float up against the ceiling,
twitching and laughing. Her formerly sweet, feminine
voice was now ragged and husky, like the time she got
strep throat, only more horrible. The voice was deep
and sharp all at once with the hint of an echo. It was not
Lacey's voice. Not at all.

"We need to get her to a doctor," Eve said. "Maybe

the opossum had rabies?"

"This is definitely not rabies!" Tina said. "Besides, opossums are marsupials! They can't give you rabies!"

"You dumb dumbs." Lacey cackled, her voice cracked and weathered. "You're too late. There's nothing you can do now."

"We have to help her!" Tina shouted. "Eve, can't you do some kind of witchy spell to bring her down?"

"I only just started learning this stuff!" Eve said. "I know as much as you do."

A terrible crunching sound filled the air as their possessed friend turned her head to the side. The snapping of bones and stretching of skin overpowered the rhythm of their beating hearts as Lacey's head continued on its unnatural trajectory. Tina screamed as Lacey's face turned toward the ceiling and rotated the full 360 degrees.

"That's it," Eve said, grabbing her purse from the floor. "I'm outie."

"No! Please don't leave!" Tina begged.

Eve wrapped her hand around the doorknob but didn't get very far.

"Ahhh!" A scream ripped from her throat as she pulled her hand away from the doorknob. Eve cradled her wrist and examined her hand, the flesh in the center of her palm already turning into a boil. Tina glanced at the door, the metallic knob now red hot.

Another sinister cackle turned their attention back to Lacey.

"You're not going anywhere," their floating friend said.

Tina glanced at her bedside table. Her untouched root beer float had somehow miraculously made it through the chaos without being overturned. She had to snap Lacey out of this state somehow. Tina lunged at the cup and grabbed it. Without giving the matter any more thought, she tossed the contents of the cup in Lacey's contorted, demonic face.

"Ayieee!" Lacey let out a garbled yell and clawed at her face. Her floating body fell to the ground as she scratched at the melted ice cream and diet root beer in her eyes. Lacey landed on the carpet face-first with a loud *THUD* and her body stilled.

"Is she ... dead?" Eve asked, peering at Lacey's lifeless form.

"Lace?" Tina asked, edging toward her friend.

Lacey gasped and pushed herself up on her arms. "What happened?"

"Oh my gosh," Tina let out a relieved breath. "You're okay."

"Why am I covered in root beer?" She asked, picking at her soaked t-shirt.

"Um, so, we may have accidentally summoned some kind of demon." Eve cringed. "But, it's okay now! You're back!"

"I'm *back*?" Lacey glanced at Tina with wide eyes. "What do you mean 'I'm back'? Where did I go?"

"You were sort of floating in the air for a while," Tina said. "Your, um, your eyes were glowing? And the room, like, was shaking and stuff."

"Oh, and your head spun all the way around," Eve said. "Sorry."

"Wait, say all that again?" Lacey scratched her head and glanced around the room. "Wow, this place is trashed."

"It was pretty scary," Eve said. "You said the name Zozo."

Lacey's head snapped back at the mention of the demon's name. Her body went rigid and a stream of neon green bile spewed from her mouth like a water fountain. Tina and Eve shielded their faces as she sprayed glowing barf around her bedroom like an automatic water sprinkler. When she was finished, the same sinister voice from before cackled deep inside their friends' throat. Lacey faced her friends with glowing eyes and a shark-toothed smile. "You called?"

"Wrong number!" Tina picked up her desk chair and held it out in front of her like a lion tamer. "Get out of my friend's body!"

"Or else what?" The demon cackled and wiped a smear of glowing barf across her cheek. "You'll tell your mommy?"

"I am so mad at Deon right now!" Eve cried.

"Poor little rookie witch," the demon said, its voice now a high-pitched mocking tone. "Your boyfriend used you, and now you have the pleasure of dealing with me."

"Eve, go get a glass of water," Tina said. "I snapped her out of this before. We can do this again."

"Wait, won't that make her melt?" Eve asked.

"She's a demon, not a witch," Tina said. "Just go get it!"

Eve rushed to the bathroom as the demon wearing Lacey's skin jumped on her bed, crouching on all fours. She growled and hissed, clawing at the bed sheets as though she were trying to dig. Her eyes flashed and made contact with Tina's gaze as she squatted over her pillow.

"Ew!" Tina gagged. "She's peeing on my bed!"

"Gross," Eve pushed a cup of tap water into Tina's hand. "Here. You're a better shot than me."

"Please, Tina. Don't do it." Lacey kneeled on the bed with her hands in prayer position, her lower lip jutting out in a pout. Her shark-like teeth were gone and her voice had returned to normal, but there was still something strange about her eyes. Tina looked at the cup and paused.

"Don't," Eve whispered. "It's a trick."

"Come on, Tiny," Lacey said. "Let's go play Barbies like we used to."

Tina's heart hurt. Whatever was happening to her best friend was because of her. If she hadn't invited them over for this stupid sleepover, none of this would have ever taken place. If she had only listened to her gut and pleaded with her friends not to mess with the dark arts, Lacey wouldn't be a walking flesh suit for some inhuman thing. She reasoned with herself that it was only a cup of water. It couldn't hurt. Tina hurled the cup at her best friend and hoped for the best.

"Psyche!" The demon cackled, dodging the spray

of water. Her body levitated again, this time hovering over the bed. "What you have summoned cannot be undone!"

"Look, our friend is gonna need her body back," Eve said. "Go crawl back to whatever corner of the underworld you came from and leave us alone."

"But I'm so *hungry*! Earth is full of so many delicious souls," the demon said. "A true buffet of awfulness. Why should I leave?"

"Because, we didn't invite you to this party," Tina said. "You're not wanted!"

"Not wanted? You mean, like how you feel not wanted by your friends?" The demon pouted. "Do you really think you ever stood a chance?"

"Okay, enough of this reverse psychology crap," Eve said. "If we brought you here, we can send you back."

"I was afraid you might say that." The demon's lips spread into a wide grin as it pointed toward the floor. The dARiA*s magazine that Tina had gotten in the mail that day floated through the air as though it were lifted by invisible hands. The demon cackled and the pages fluttered back and forth as a rush of warm air filled the room.

"We need to get something to tie her down," Eve

said. "Like a rope. Something to bind her hands."

"What about this?" Tina held up an elastic hair tie.

"No, something to really hold her down. I need to go find Deon and get him to help us reverse this," Eve said. "Maybe we can trap her in the bathroom?"

"I guess we have to try," Tina said. "I'll get her left side, you get the right?"

"On three," Eve said. "One, two, three!"

Eve and Tina lunged for the levitating demon. Tina grabbed her right arm and Eve went for the right. They pulled and they pulled, but it was nearly impossible to bring the creature down.

"Hang on!" The demon cackled.

Before they could react, the demon spun in a circle in midair with Eve and Tina holding on for dear life. Tina maintained her grip for one rotation before being flung into the dresser. Eve continued to try and pull her to the floor with little effect. Finally, the demon stopped spinning long enough to raise her left hand and bring a set of claws down on Eve's arm.

"Ahhh!"

Eve let go and grabbed her forearm.

"I've got big plans," the demon said. "It'll take more than two pathetic little girls to stop me."

"We're not going to let you have our friend!" Eve said.

"It's too late," the demon cackled. "Her soul is mine."

The pages of the dELiA*s catalog flipped furiously back and forth again. The demon pointed her left hand at Tina and her right hand at Eve.

"You two are a real trip," the demon said. "But our time together is at an end. Goodbye."

Tina felt something tug at her chest as her heels rose up from the floor. She was being pulled toward her bed and the flipping pages of her favorite catalog.

"Eve!" She screamed. "What's going on?"

"I don't know!" Eve shouted. "I can't move my legs!"

Tina's sixteenth birthday flashed before her eyes as her body continued to be dragged. It had been a nearly perfect party up until they started playing games they had no business getting into. Now she was under the control of some messed up demon who looked like her best friend, with no way of helping her. Tina's head snapped back as she was pulled further and further until she couldn't move at all and her entire world was bathed in white.

Chapter Nine

"**H**Ey GuRL! wHaT hApPeNEd tO yOu?"

Tina sat up and rubbed her eyes, temporarily blinded by a wall-to-wall world of white. Her head spun as she was helped to her feet by a cool, slim hand. She squinted as her blurred vision cleared, and as she regained focus, it became obvious that she was no longer in her room.

"cUtE tOp, bABe!" A feminine voice said. "wHeRe DiD yOu GeT iT?"

Tina blinked as she glanced around the blank canvas that was now her world. The voice and hand belonged to the most gorgeous, coolest girl she had ever seen in her life. Her chestnut hair was cut in a sleek bob and pinned to one side with a plastic baby barrette. Dark, wide eyes peeped out from under thick lashes that fluttered against an impossibly adorable spray of freckles. Her oversized blue v-neck sweater looked comfortable and cool paired with equally baggy wide-wale corduroy pants, but it was the rainbow-soled platform sandals that really tied the look together. Tina stared down at her own less than fashionable outfit and the *No Fear* t-shirt she had gotten from Lacey.

"Oh, um. My best friend gave this shirt to me. For my sixteenth birthday."

"YoUr BiRtHdAy!" The girl exclaimed. "hApPy SwEeT sIxTeEn!"

"Thanks," Tina glanced over her shoulder. There was nothing around but white, white and more white as far as she could see. "Where am I?"

"wInTeR '96, pAgE 13." the girl nodded. "Racer v-neck sweater, $29. Corduroy hipster jeans, $39. Platform flip-flops, $19. Plastic bow baby barrette 12-pack, $6."

Gooseflesh prickled up and down Tina's arms. She remembered where she had seen this girl before. "Wait. Are you a model for dARiA*s?"

"dARiA*s?" The girl asked. "wHaT*s tHaT?"

"Tina!" Eve's voice echoed through the white void. "Where are you?"

"That's my friend," Tina said. "Can you help me find her?"

"I LoVe FrIeNds!" The girl said. "CoMe On, I cAn TaKe YoU tO mEeT mInE!"

The girl took her hand and led her through the world of white, down a white corridor. Her flip-flops made an echoey *thwack, thwack, thwack* sound as Tina struggled to keep up with the energetic girl. They turned the corner past a wall of shoes and tights set against a stark white background.

sTaY sWeEt aLL wInTeR

Platform mary janes, $49

Hot pink combat boots, $79

Suede clogs, $59

Opaque tights, $19

Striped tights, $24

Knit pompom beanie, $19

"What the hell is this?" Tina mused as they passed another wall of home decor items.

yOuR rOoM, yOuR rULeS

Inflatable sofa, $49

Moon and stars beaded curtain, $26

Lava lamp, $29

Alien throw pillow, $19

Hot pink shag rug, $39

"Hey, I have that rug," Tina said, a chill running down her spine. The further and further they ventured into the white maze, the more clear her situation became. She was inside her favorite magazine. Somehow, the demon had sent her there. Or trapped her there. She didn't know which one was worse.

"hUrRy uP!" The girl said, tugging her hand. "aLmOsT tHeRe!"

Every time they turned a corner, the sound of a flipping page echoed through the void. Even though she had spent so many hours lovingly dog-earing pages and circling items in this very catalog, she didn't want to actually be stuck in it. She had spent so many birthdays and holidays wishing she could have everything in this catalog at her fingertips. She should have known to be careful what you wish for. At that moment, all she wanted to do was find her friend, get back home and figure out how to help Lacey. They turned another corner and a wave of relief washed over Tina when she spotted Eve around the corner, surrounded by a half dozen other teen girls.

"IsN*t ShE sO pReTty?" A girl in a satin babydoll dress cooed.

"Oh, I jUsT lOvE yOuR gOtH lOoK!" Another girl with pigtail braids wearing a pair of floral flannel pajamas chimed in.

"Eve!" Tina ran to her friend and greeted her with a big hug. "What is happening?"

"Oh my goddess," Eve said, staring at Tina with wide eyes. "Can you make them stop talking like this?"

Tina turned to the v-neck sweater girl. "Is there, um … Do you guys always talk like this?"

"LiKe WhAt?" Another girl with a monkey print baby t-shirt and oversized, wide-leg jeans asked.

"Nevermind." Tina cringed.

"She wants us to turn off the varying upper and lower cases when we speak," another girl said. She was dressed in denim overalls and a pink tank top. Two space buns sat on top of her head secured with matching pink marabou hair ties. "You two must be new here. I'm Elaine."

"Jasmine!" The girl in the satin babydoll dress said.

"I'm Mariella," the pajama girl said.

"Alyssa," waved the girl in the monkey print tee.

"Kassie," the v-neck sweater girl said.

Tina turned to Eve. "We're in the catalog."

"The dARiA*'s catalog?"

Tina nodded.

"How?" Eve crossed her arms at her chest. "How is this possible?"

"Your guess is as good as mine."

"Dammit, Deon," Eve reached into her purse and pulled out her notebook. "I knew I shouldn't have trusted him."

Tina turned to Elaine, the space buns girl. "We need to get home. Can you help us?"

Elaine shrugged. "This *is* our home."

"So, you're trapped here too?"

"We're not trapped!" Mariella said, hugging a stuffed animal. "We're hanging with our best friends. Every day is a slumber party."

"You only say that because you get to wear pajamas," Jasmine said, tugging at the hem of her satin dress. "I can't even properly bend over in this thing."

"You can put on a pair of pajamas if you want," Elaine said. "It's not like we don't have a bunch of them."

Tina exchanged a worried look with Eve as the cat-alog girls bickered. She grabbed the skin on her forearm with her thumb and forefinger and pinched hard. "Ow."

"So, this is real." Eve said. "We're not hallucinating from too much sugar or caffeine or something?"

"Seems like it," Tina said. "If Deon got us into this, can you think of anything he said to get us out?"

"There might be something in here," Eve said, flipping through her notebook. "Incantations, Curses, Binding Spells ... Oh, right here! Spell reversals."

"Spells!" Kassie jumped for joy and clapped. "Oh, I love witchy stuff!"

"This says we need to collect the same items we used to cast the spell in order to reverse it," Eve said. "I don't remember using any items though."

"Candles!" Tina said. "You lit a bunch of candles, didn't you?"

"Oh yeah," Eve glanced up at the catalog girls. "You guys have any candles around here?"

The catalog girls gazed at each other with conspiratorial smiles.

"Definitely," Elaine said. "Ladies, let's give them the grand tour."

Over the next few hours, Tina and Eve were led down a fashion bender rabbit hole as the catalog girls threw new clothes and accessories at them. Jelly shoes. Choker necklaces. Body glitter. Butterfly hair clips. Beaded cardigans. Board shorts. Peasant tops. Cargo skirts. Bikinis. They tried on anything and everything the catalog world had to offer. It was the ultimate trip to the mall. The best makeover ever. The best girls trip ever.

But with each pullover sweater, messenger bag, or pair of novelty socks they wore, Tina and Eve were sucked further and further away from their goal. By the time they had tried on everything that the Winter '96 catalog had to offer, the two friends had forgotten all about Lacey. They forgot about Tina's birthday party demon. They forgot about their friends and family, about going back home, about starting school that following Monday. The catalog wasn't just a place where fashion dreams were kept; it was a place where people were sent to be forgotten.

Chapter Ten

Tina was floating on a pink cloud of teenage day-dreams. In the world of white, nothing mattered anymore; she didn't care about what other people thought of her, or about going back to school, or getting her driver's license. She didn't care about her mother or best friends or secret crushes. She forgot about Lacey, about her birthday party and what she and Eve had done. Within those blindingly white, fashionable walls, Tina retreated inside herself, indulging in all of her fantasies.

The latest album from *No Doubt* played through glittery purple speakers as the catalog girls whisked Tina and Eve through the winding halls of the catalog. Each room felt like a different specialty store, each set within a labyrinth of white. That room is for shoes. That room is for dresses. That room is for bathing suits. Time stood still as Tina and Eve were handed an endless parade of hangers dripping with beautiful clothes in shiny spandex, soft leather and plush velvet.

With every outfit they tried on, Tina forgot herself and the world a little bit more. In a way, this was what she had always wanted — a way to escape the monotony of life. She and Eve had endless fashion options at their fingertips and a new group of girlfriends to hang out with. The catalog girls were who she had always dreamed of becoming; cool, stylish, fun. Within these white walls, every day was an endless sleepover, an endless summer, an endless trip to the mall with the girls.

"yOuR nEw LeWk iS sO rAd!" Elaine gushed, wrapping a pink feather boa around Tina's neck.

"tHaNkS," Tina cooed, reapplying a layer of bubblegum pink gloss to her lips. "eVe, wHaT dO yOu ThInK oF tHiS cOLoR?"

"sO hOt," Eve said, admiring her metallic blue manicure.

"yOu GuRlz sEtTLe iN," Elaine said, flashing them a peace sign. "g2g aNc cHeCk oN tHe oThEr GuRlz.

BRB!"

"bYeEeE!" Eve said, flopping into a pink inflatable armchair.

"hEy, cHeCk oUt ThEsE sWeEt SuNnIeS." Tina passed a pair of white vintage pin-up style sunglasses to Eve to try on.

"tHaNkS, GuRl."

Eve took the sunglasses from Tina and slid them up the bridge of her nose. She had switched out her goth girl attire for a pair of brown satin cargo pants, a strappy cranberry colored camisole and suede skateboard sneakers. In the background, the catalog girls jumped and posed, did cartwheels, made funny faces at each other, and giggled amongst themselves.

"tHaNkS, gUrL." Eve pushed the sunglasses up the bridge of her nose.

Tina spun around in a circle, entranced by the hem of her orange retro-print shirt dress as it fluttered above the knee. She admired the white patent leather platform shoes that Kassie had given her to wear, perfect paired with frilly ankle socks from Jasmine. Elaine had parted her hair in the middle and fashioned her lackluster locks into pigtails that hung above her shoulders. Tina walked over to the makeup wall, grabbed a compact mirror, and admired her reflection. She didn't look like herself anymore. She looked like a catalog girl.

"eVe, DoEs ThIs SeEm WeI—" Tina cleared her throat. "Does this seem weird to you?"

"wHaT dO yOu MeAn, GuRL?"

"We're talking like them!" Tina whispered. "And dressing like them!"

The plastic chair made a squeaky sound as Eve stood up and shook her head. She stared down at her feet and gagged. "Ew. Am I wearing *sneakers*?"

"I think they're trying to stall us," Tina whispered.

Eve lowered the sunglasses from the bridge of her nose and tugged Tina's sleeve. "I think you're right."

Tina followed Eve's gaze to where the catalog girls were huddled on the far end of the white room. One by one, the catalog girls turned to face them, their eyes blazing bright. Glowing like Lacey's did back in her bedroom.

Their new "friends" weren't catalog models.

They were demons.

"Eve," Tina said, her breath catching in her throat. "I think it's time for us to peace out."

Chapter Eleven

In a world of white, there was nowhere for them to run, and nowhere for them to hide. Tina and Eve fled through the blinding catalog maze anyway, followed by a horde of fashionable, demonic teenage girls.

"hEy GuRl, wHeRe U gOiN*?"

"dOn*T bE a DrAg!"

"wE jUsT wAnNa eAt YoUr SoUl!"

Tina and Eve scrambled through the corridor pages of the Winter '96 catalog past puffy jackets, pom-pom hats, oversized snowboard sweaters and chunky heeled boots. Tina nearly wiped out against a display of Christmas pajamas featuring cartoon characters with matching plush slippers. Eve helped Tina to her feet as the sound of pages flipping echoed against the white walls and the seasonal style on the racks changed from cozy knits in red and green to plaid and corduroy in orange, brown and rust. They ran back in time toward the Fall '95 back-to-school catalog featuring funky mini backpacks, knee-high socks to wear with plaid mini skirts and baby tees. The sound of platform sandals and sneakers pounded behind them as Tina wracked her brain in search of somewhere to hide. Finally, they came upon a wall that said yOuR dOrM iS sO rAd, with a real bedroom set display.

Groovy floral twin comforter, $59

Baby pink twin sheet set, $29

True love candles, $13

Good night bath salts and sleep mask gift set, $19

"Over there," Tina said. "Let's hide under the bed."

"Don't you think they'll know we're hiding there?" Eve asked.

"They don't seem very bright to me," Tina said. "We have to try."

"Okay, fine. Just don't let them eat our souls."

They slid on their bellies under the bed and waited as the parade of demonic catalog models caught up to them. Their high-pitched giggles echoed through the white walled space as they continued on their trajectory, not even bothering to stop.

Tina exhaled in relief as their voices disappeared into the distance. "Now what?"

"Now we figure out how to reverse this spell," Eve said. She retrieved the notebook from her purse and flipped it open. "Well, I'm glad we ended up on this page. Most of the items we need are right here."

"What do we need?" Tina whispered.

"Candles, since I lit them to start the spell. A mirror to reflect and reverse the spell. Totems of our friendship. Oh, and salt."

"What's the salt for?"

"Protection."

Eve slipped out from under the bed first. She grabbed one of the candles from the bedside table as well as the jar of bath salts. Tina glanced around the space for a sign of other supplies they could use, but came up empty.

"There was a mirror in the last room we were in," Tina said. "By the makeup."

"Okay," Eve glanced over her shoulder. "We should hurry in case they come back. Take off your shoes, those things are loud."

Tina slipped out of her platform shoes and Eve unlaced her sneakers. They stashed the shoes under the bed and took off in the opposite direction of the catalog demons. They raced past rows of satin bomber jackets, purple peacoats and faux fur shrugs, past walls of graphic print baby tees, slouchy oversized denim and mini backpack purses. Finally, they reached the place where they had begun and faced a wall of pastel nail polishes, mood color change lipsticks, and eye-opening eyeshadows.

"Mirrored compact," Tina said, grabbing two from the wall. "Got it. Now what?"

"We need a totem," Eve said. "Something that represents us. Something that ties us all together."

Tina and Eve locked eyes, and said the same thing at the same time. "Best friend necklaces."

"I think there was a wall of jewelry by the accessories section," Eve said.

"Let's go."

The two friends were off again, whizzing through the world of white, surrounded by a seemingly never ending supply of consumerist goods. A wall of dresses in floral, gingham, stripe, and polka dot patterns flew by, giving way to another wall of denim shorts in a rainbow of colors, sizes and shapes. Novelty telephones. Purple CD players. A pink Hello Kitty television with a built-in VHS player. Everything a teen girl could ever want was within reach, and it was all theirs for the taking. It would have been so easy for Tina to forget about her troubles at home, to stay in this neverland of dress-up and endless teen girl dreams. But she had to get back to Lacey. She had to make this right. That's what a best friend would do.

"There. By the purses," Eve said, as they entered another white room.

Tina followed her to a wall of jewelry. Peace sign earrings, yin-yang necklaces, plastic rainbow rings and smiley face pendants lined the wall. There were pewter rings with stars and moons, mood rings, plastic bracelets, and hundreds of glittery, jewel studded barrettes. Finally, next to the row of puka shell necklaces, Tina spotted what she was looking for.

"Eve! I got it!" Tina picked out a charm bracelet busting with dozens of enamel charms; cats, a sun, ice cream, and most importantly, Best Friends Forever heart charms.

"Perfect. Get three of those charms," Eve said. "Now that we have the totems, all we need to do is recite the spell."

"hEy! wHeRe Do YoU tHiNk YoU*rE gOiNg?"

Tina's blood chilled as the sound of cackling teenage girls and shrieking demons echoed through the white void walls. The catalog demons were coming. They were too late.

Tina and Eve turned and gasped as a horde of trendy teens appeared from behind a white wall, filling the space of the jewelry and accessories section. Dozens of gorgeous girls in pink halter tops, spaghetti strap sundresses, flower power bikinis and smiley face t-shirts grinned at them with sharp teeth and glowing eyes. Tina gulped, knowing that reasoning with them was likely out of the question, but she had to try anyway.

"We need to go help our friend," Tina said. "Don't try to stop us."

"bUt We*Re YoUr FrIeNds NoW," Elaine said, her lips set in a shark-like smile.

"Distract them," Eve whispered.

"Hey, did you ever realize that the sizes in this catalog are a little limiting?" Tina said. "Where are all the plus sizes anyway?"

"wE*rE dEmOnS," Kassie said, rolling her glowing eyes. "wE*rE nOt TrYiNg tO bE iNcLuSiVe, dUh."

"You know, all I ever wanted was to have all the cool things in this catalog," Tina said. "Now that I have it, I can see all of this stuff for what it really is."

"aNd WhAt*s ThAt?" Jasmine said, her eyes aglow.

"It's all just a bunch of junk."

Eve unscrewed the top of the bath salts and sent a spray of nighttime bath elixir flying through the air. The model demons screeched and recoiled as the scented bath salts hit their skin. Circular pockets of flesh sizzled and melted away as the salt touched their exposed skin. As they screamed and writhed, Eve used the remaining salt to form a protective circle around her and Tina.

"Quick, Eve! We have to finish this." Tina clutched the BFF charms in one hand and the mirrors in the other, her anxiety climbing.

Eve stuck her hand in her purse, her features pinched as she frantically rummaged around. "I can't find my lighter! I don't have anything to light the candle! The incantation won't work!"

"We have to try," Tina said. "We don't have any other choice."

"Okay. Give me a mirror and a charm." Eve sat the candle in the center of the circle and launched into a chant. "*What once was done, now undo. Take back the spell we cast, times two."*

Tina winced as the demon models yowled on the outskirts of their circle. Splotches of skin fell away from their face where the salt had hit them, revealing ghoulish, sinewy features beneath. At that moment, Tina vowed to stock up on all of the bath salts she could find at Bath & Body Works when she got home.

"Eve?" She asked. "Is it working?"

"I don't know," she said, flipping through her notebook. "Oh! We have to say the spell in reverse. The one that got us here?"

"We didn't say a spell though?"

"Yes we did," Eve said. "Take my hand and repeat after me."

Tina gulped as the demon models edged nearer. Would the salt circle hold out long enough? Would this plan even work?

"Board a as stiff, feather a as light," Eve said.

"What?"

"I know it doesn't roll off the tongue, just stay with me here!" Eve said.

Tina took a deep breath and chanted along with her friend.

"Board a as stiff, feather a as light."

"Board a as stiff, feather a as light."

"Board a as stiff, feather a as light."

"Board a as stiff, feather a as light."

A cool breeze fluttered through the air. The scent of cinnamon and sunshine. Lacey.

"It's going to work!" Tina exclaimed.

"Good!" Eve shouted. "Now shut up and keep chanting!"

"Board a as stiff, feather a as light."

"Board a as stiff, feather a as light."

"Board a as stiff, feather a as light."

"Board a as stiff, feather a as light."

The cool breeze intensified, swirling around Eve and Tina like a vortex. The wind lifted bath salt particles into the air, stinging at the demon models' flesh. Their screeches tore through Tina's brain. She squeezed her eyes shut as they attempted to cross the salt circle threshold.

"Board a as stiff, feather a as light."

"Board a as stiff, feather a as light."

"Board a as stiff, feather a as light."

"Board a as stiff, feather a as light."

"Board a as stiff, feather a as light."

"Board a as stiff, feather a as light."

"Board a as stiff, feather a as light."

"Board a as stiff, feather a as light."

A demon model reached out and scratched Tina's arm. A searing pain ripped at her flesh, but she continued chanting.

"Board a as stiff, feather a as light."

"Board a as stiff, feather a as light."

"Board a as stiff, feather a as light."

"Board a as stiff, feather a as light."

The cold wind howled around them now, creating a cyclone of polyester, satin, and lace. Slip-on sneakers, stuffed animals, imitation jewelry, makeup, and flirty dresses flew by as the demon models were flung into the air.

"Board a as stiff, feather a as light."

"Board a as stiff, feather a as light."

"Board a as stiff, feather a as light."

"Board a as stiff, feather a as light."

"Eve! I'm sorry I doubted you!" Tina called out. "You'll always be my best friend!"

"I'm sorry too!"

A great roar filled the air as Tina felt her feet lift from the ground. She was carried up, up, and away through the tornado of clothes. The world in white vanished,

and all she knew was a dark black void and nothing
more.

95

Chapter Twelve

"**W**ake up, sleepyhead. Time for your birthday breakfast!"

Bright sunlight streamed in through the blinds of Tina's bedroom window as she struggled to open her eyes. She was back home, safe in her bed, and everything hurt from her head all the way down to her toes. Eve stirred at the foot of her bed, wrapped in a comforter-like a cocoon with only her long, dark hair poking out. Tina sat up and her world spun all around as the events from the night before came back into focus.

The Ouija board.

Lacey.

The demon.

Tina glanced around her bedroom expecting to see evidence of the carnage from the night before. There should have been neon demon bodily fluids all over the floor, her belongings scattered like the aftermath of a hurricane. But other than the cracked glass on the picture frame on her dresser, everything was in its place, just as it should be, but Lacey was nowhere to be found.

"My *head*," Eve moaned and rolled over. "What happened?"

"Did we ... Did you?" Tina picked up the dARiA*s magazine from her bedside table. "Did you have the same messed up dream I had?"

Eve tore off the comforter and gasped. She was still dressed in the tomboy skater clothes that the demon models gave her. Tina glanced down at herself to see that she was still dressed in the retro print shirt dress from the catalog, too. She flipped through the pages of the catalog, instantly recognizing the faces smiling back at her. Jasmine. Kassie. Elaine. They were all there, fashionably frozen in time in a world of white.

"O. M. G." Tina launched out of bed, threw open her door, and called out to her mother. "Hey, did you see Lacey leave?"

"Yeah, she left just a few minutes ago. Said she had

to go home." Her mother poked her head out into the hallway. "You want whipped cream on your pancakes?"

"No thanks. I'm not hungry," Tina said.

"That's a cute dress," her mother said, waving a spatula in her direction. "Did Lacey get you that for your birthday too?"

"I guess she did." A sinking feeling wormed its way into Tina's gut. Was it all just a dream? Tina picked up the phone on her bedside table and punched her number into the clear handset by memory. The phone only rang once before Lacey's mother picked up.

"Tina! Happy birthday."

"Thanks, Mrs. Dennison." Tina twirled the cord around her finger, her stomach lurching. "Is Lacey there?"

"She got home a little bit ago, thanks for checking in. You gals must have stayed up super late. She just flopped into bed and crashed!"

"We did," Tina said. "Okay, thanks."

"Bye now."

Tina returned her phone to the receiver and turned to face Eve. She had already slipped out of the skater clothes and back into a black lace dress she had brought for the sleepover.

"Brown pants? Seriously? What was I thinking?"

"They didn't look that bad," Tina said. "What's that on your arm?"

Eve sat up and examined her forearm. A swollen red scratch ran down the length of it from her elbow to her wrist. "This is where Lacey scratched me."

"So, last night. That was all real?"

"I guess so," Eve said, lacing up her combat boots. "What time is it?"

Tina glanced at her purple digital clock. "Almost noon."

"Good. The video store should be open by now." Eve grabbed the rented VHS tapes from on top of Tina's television. "Deon has some explaining to do."

Thirty minutes later, Tina and Eve pulled up in front of Cool Flix with their VHS return tapes in hand. Tina forced herself to look at her reflection in the mirrored windows as they walked in. The mass that had been hovering over her the past few days was gone, transferred to Lacey perhaps. Maybe it had all just been in her mind to begin with. "There's no way that we could have a shared delusion, right?" Tina asked as Eve opened the door to Cool Flix. "Like, we couldn't have both had the same freaky dream, right?"

"What happened last night was real," Eve said. "And we're going to get Deon to help us fix it."

Eve marched up to the front counter of the video store. Deon stood behind the register with his back to them, rewinding video tapes in a machine. Eve slammed the tapes on the countertop and smirked as Deon's shoulders jumped. He turned around to face them, his eyes wide in surprise.

"Oh, hey. You scared me."

"Deon, what was in that spell you taught me?" Eve glared at him, her arms crossed over her chest. "We need you to help us undo it. *Now.*"

"What spell?"

"You know." Eve hissed and lowered her voice. "The floating spell. Light as a feather?"

"Oh. That one." Deon cringed. "You didn't really do it, did you?"

"Yes! I told you I was going to!" Eve said. "And it worked. Too well. Lacey is, like, possessed with some Zo demon or something."

"She was floating on my ceiling and puking up high-lighter green slime," Tina said. "Her eyes were *glowing*. We need your help."

"Wait." Deon held up his hands, his expression grave. "Did you also mess around with a Ouija board?"

"Yeah," Eve said. "Why?"

"Was the demon named Zoz—"

"Don't say its name!" Tina shushed him, waving her hands. "I think it gets more power when you say its name or something."

"Dude, I don't know what to tell you," Deon said, scratching the back of his neck. "Ras said not to mix that spell with anything else. Did you say her eyes were *glowing*?"

"Yes! That's what we're trying to tell you," Eve said, exasperated. "Our friend is possessed because of your dumb spell and now we need to reverse it."

"Okay, hold up. Lemme call Ras and see if he knows anything." Deon picked up the Cool Flix phone and punched in a few numbers.

"Ras?" Tina asked.

"Rasputin." Eve rolled her eyes. "His real name is Tyler. He just calls himself Rasputin to seem mysterious and cool."

"Oh."

After a minute, the phone rang back and Deon picked it up. "Thank you for calling Cool Flix. How can I help you? Ras, hey man. We've got a problem."

Tina reached into the pocket of her dress as Deon spoke on the phone. Her hand closed around a small metallic item. She pulled it out to reveal her portion of the BFF charm. A lump rose in her throat as she thought about Lacey. Her best friend. The person she loved most in the whole world. Where was she? Was she going to be okay?

"Thanks, dude. Okay, Bye." Deon hung up the phone and faced Eve and Tina. "Okay, so Ras thinks we can get this fixed tonight. You just need to bring your friend down to the cemetery on old US-41 and meet us around 9 p.m. We have to do this thing under a full moon, but well before midnight or it will be too late. Oh, and don't forget to bring the Ouija board."

"I'm not messing with that thing again," Eve said. "There's got to be another way."

"Nope. You invited this Zo— this *demon* — into your friend's body through the spirit board. You wanna get it out, you need the spirit board to send it back to where it came from."

"Great. I'm going to spend the first night after my sixteenth birthday in a graveyard with a Ouija board and some guy named after a weird old dude." Tina groaned. "You're sure this is the only way to help Lacey?"

Eve and Deon exchanged worried glances.

"I don't know of any other way." Deon shrugged.

"How are we going to get Lacey to come with us?" Tina asked. "She was so scary last night. I don't think she'll come willingly."

"Even if she wasn't possessed by some Ouija board demon, she probably wouldn't come with us to a graveyard at night," Eve said. "But we have to try."

"Here," Deon pulled a black JanSport backpack onto the counter. Pentagrams, band logos and other symbols were drawn all over it in whiteout ink. He unzipped the backpack and pulled out a thick leather-bound book with yellowed pages. "You can borrow this, but I'm gonna need it back. There should be some demon trapping spells in there."

"More spells?" Eve sighed. "This is like homework. I thought witchcraft was supposed to be fun."

"How do we know she's still possessed?" Tina glanced at Deon. "Seriously, what if we just had too much sugar and it was all a bad dream?"

"We woke up wearing clothes from the catalog! Besides, does this look real enough to you?" Eve rubbed at the scratch on her forearm. "Ow."

"Good point," Tina said. "That actually looks pretty bad."

"It's getting worse." Eve nodded. "I think it's infected."

"Maybe you should see a doctor or something?"

"I'll be fine." Eve pursed her lips. "Are you okay?"

Tina shook her head and her throat tightened. "What if this doesn't work? What if Lacey really is possessed and we screw up again?"

Eve turned to Deon with a narrowed, piercing gaze. "Oh, it will work. It *has* to."

Chapter Thirteen

The lingering scent of breakfast pancakes and maple syrup greeted Tina and Eve as they returned to Eve's house later that afternoon. Her mother had left a note for her on the kitchen table that said, *'Gone to the mall! Pancakes are in the oven. Love you, Mom XOXO.'* Tina knew that a trip to the mall for her mother meant she would likely have the house to herself for a long time. It was a good thing too; she and Eve needed time to prepare.

Tina's stomach grumbled as the two friends helped themselves to a plate of pancakes. They sat down at the kitchen table, physically and emotionally exhausted from the events over the last twenty-four hours. Eve grabbed the book that Deon let them borrow and began to read.

"This thing is like reading a textbook," Eve sighed. "So many old words."

"Where did Deon even get that from?" Tina asked.

"Not sure. It's really old, though. Okay, right here, it says salt and iron can help to trap demonic spirits," Eve said between bites of pancake. "Isn't the cemetery surrounded by a metal gate?"

"Yes. Plus it's, like, holy land, so demons aren't powerful there, right?" Tina poked at her uneaten pancake.

"Sure, I guess." Eve turned the page of the leatherbound book. "So, once we get her to the cemetery, she can't leave and we'll be able to perform the reversal ceremony. It's just getting her there that's the problem."

"What about salt?" Tina picked up the salt shaker on her kitchen counter. "That worked to keep the catalog model demons away."

"Yeah, but it would take a lot of salt to make a boundary around her," Eve said. "Okay, right here it says you can draw this symbol and trap a demon. It can be drawn on a door, a floor, or a pair of restraints."

Tina glanced over Eve's shoulder at the illustration on the page. In the illustration, a man in a robe stood over a woman with her hands bound together. The woman was curled up in a ball on the floor in the center of a giant pentagram.

"So, we need to make demon trap handcuffs?"

Eve nodded. "It says here that if we slip a bracelet over her wrist that bears this symbol, we should be able to control her."

"For how long?"

Eve shrugged. "For as long as the symbol remains intact. Do you have anything we could use?"

A lightbulb went off over Tina's head. "I'll be right back."

After a moment, Tina returned from her bedroom with a white fabric scrunchie and a black permanent marker.

"What are you going to do with that? Style her hair?" Eve snorted.

"No! I can draw the symbol onto the fabric with a permanent marker," Tina said. "Then we just have to slip it on her wrist, and voila!"

"That might work." Eve pursed her lips. "Wait, there's one more thing. Right here it says that as the demon becomes more human, it becomes even more powerful and less susceptible to the trap."

"That doesn't sound good." Tina frowned. "We don't have much time, do we?"

"Nope."

"Okay then," Tina said, forking a big bite of pancake. "Looks like we got a demon to trap."

"Come on in, girls. She's been sleeping all day!"

It was later that afternoon when the mother of their possessed friend answered the door for them. The setting sun chased them all the way to Lacey's house, blanketing their little town in an unsettling quiet. Time was running out. There was a sparkle in Mrs. Dennison's eyes and an empty wine glass in her hand, and for a brief moment, Tina realized they might be able to pull off their plan. Sneaking Lacey out of the house may just work after all.

Tina and Eve entered the Dennison home armed with demon trapping paraphernalia and their best fake smiles. They had a loose idea of how they were going to get Lacey out of the house and down to the cemetery in time to meet Deon and Rasputin. Whether or not

Lacey's mother was relaxed enough to let them take her was another matter.

"Tina, did you have a nice birthday?" Mrs. Dennison covered her mouth and gave a small hiccup as she swayed on her feet.

"Oh, I sure did, Mrs. Dennison," Tina said, hitching her backpack over her shoulder. "Thanks for letting Lacey stay the night."

"You girls are all growing up so fast," Mrs. Dennison said, her voice slightly slurred. "You can go on into her room. She might still be sleeping. She's been so tired all day!"

"Thank you, Mrs. D." Eve flashed Lacey's mother a megawatt smile as the two girls walked through Lacey's home. They reached her bedroom door with her softball team's pennant tacked to the outside.

Tina glanced at Eve and took a deep breath. "Ready?"

Eve nodded. "Let's go get our friend."

Tina gently rapped on the door. "Lace? It's us. Can we come in?"

Nothing. Eve reached for the knob and went to open the door and then thought twice. She glanced down at the palm of her hand, a circular burn mark still there from the night before.

"You open the door this time," Eve said. "I don't have such great luck with doorknobs."

"Okay," Tina said. "Here goes nothing."

Tina tapped at the doorknob, relieved to find it cool to the touch. She gently turned the knob so as not to make any noise and slowly opened the door. What she saw next confirmed all of her fears.

Lacey hovered a foot over her bed, still clothed in the outfit she wore the day before. A blanket hung off her body like a shroud as she took in labored, gurgling breaths. Her eyes were closed, and it appeared as though she was sleeping.

"Hey, Lace? Uh, it's us. How you doin'?" Tina unzipped the front pocket of her backpack and pulled out the scrunchie.

A warm breeze blew through Tina's room. Photos tacked to the corkboard over her desk fluttered and a low groan filled the air.

"We need to act fast." Tina reached into the backpack and pulled out a container of salt. "Spread this in a circle just in case."

"On it." Eve snapped the metallic spout of the salt container open and began to pour.

A low whine rang in her ears, and Tina's blood ran cold as she glanced up at her floating friend. Lacey stared back at her with glowing eyes and lips spread open wide to reveal rows of sharp teeth.

"What's up, witches?"

"Oh, crap." Eve finished her salt circle and held the container out like a weapon. "Tina! Get over here!"

"Salt is smart, but it will take more than that to contain me," Lacey said in that same demonic voice. "Won't be much longer now."

"Listen you sucky ass demon," Tina said, her voice shaking. "It's our first day back at school tomorrow and our friend needs her body back, like *now*."

"Well, why don't you come and take it?" Lacey reached out a hand, her glowing eyes locked onto Tina. Her once perfectly manicured pink nails were now long, sharp talons tinged black and green.

"I think I will." Tina gathered all of her courage, all of her will and stretched the elastic of the scrunchie as wide as it could go. In one swift move, she placed the scrunchie marked with the demon trap insignia onto the wrist of her possessed friend. A demonic scream ripped from her throat as Eve pulled Tina back into the salt circle. Lacey's body went limp and fell to the bed as the glowing light left her eyes.

"Did it work?" Tina panted, holding tight to Eve.

Eve took a tentative step toward Lacey's bed. She reached out a hand and poked her leg. Lacey didn't move. "I think so."

"Okay. What now?" Tina asked, glancing at her watch. It was already late and Deon and Ras were waiting.

Eve picked up a pair of sunglasses from Lacey's dresser and gave Tina a knowing look. "Now we give her the *Weekend at Bernie's* treatment, sneak her out of here and send that demon back to board game hell."

The two friends worked quietly, dressing Lacey's limp body. They eased her favorite Looney Tunes hoodie over her head, and Tina flinched at Bugs Bunny and Tweety as they gazed at her with their bug-eyed stares. Eve found a pair of slip-on checkered Vans and eased them onto Lacey's feet like some kind of messed up Cinderella. Tina carefully placed the sunglasses on her face and wiped a smudge of green crust from the corner of her mouth. Even possessed by a demon, Tina thought her friend was beautiful.

"This will have to do," Eve said.

"Now what?" Tina's gut lurched.

"Now we take her to my car." Eve shrugged.

"Shouldn't we try to smuggle her out or something?" Tina hitched her thumb toward the window. "Wouldn't that be easier?"

"Nah. Her mom will freak out if she sees that she's gone," Eve said. "Better to pretend that we are taking her somewhere."

"Do you really think her mom will just let us take Lacey out of here? On a school night?"

"We'll make something up," Eve said. "I've seen her mom like this before. She won't care."

"If you say so."

"Okay, just like that time Lacey twisted her ankle playing kickball," Eve said, throwing one of Lacey's limp arms over her shoulder. "You get the other side."

Tina grabbed Lacey's other arm, the girl's body heavy and limp. Together, Tina and Eve managed to whisk their unconscious friend down the hall toward the front door.

"Thanks so much for letting us take her to the mall, Mrs. D. My dad sent me birthday money for back to school clothes, and well, Lacey always has the best taste." Tina forced a huge smile as she held onto Lacey's left arm.

"Have fun, girls! Just be back by ten. You have school tomorrow!" Lacey's mom said, a glass of wine in one hand and the television remote in the other.

"Will do, Mrs. D!" Eve said, hoisting Lacey's body up on the right side.

Lacey's head tilted forward, the sunglasses almost sliding off the bridge of her nose as they hoisted her out the front door. With a hoodie on, a pair of slip-on shoes and a pair of sunglasses, their friend was passable enough to get through the door. Most parents would have been suspicious, but, thankfully for them, Mrs. Dennison had worked most of the way through a bottle of chardonnay.

"She's so much heavier than she looks!" Eve grunted as they shuffled toward her car. "It's a good thing we love her."

"It's just all the muscle from playing softball," Tina said. "Anyway, don't make fun of her, especially since we accidentally got her possessed!"

"I'm not making fun! Just sayin', this isn't easy," Eve said. "Okay, I'm going to open the trunk."

"The trunk!"

"Do you really want to be stuck in the car with her if this demon trap stops working?" Eve asked, popping the trunk.

"Good point."

"Okay, together now," Eve said. "One, two, three. Oof!"

Tina and Eve unloaded Lacey's body into the back of her Dodge Neon. She looked so peaceful and still, and for a moment, Tina practically forgot that a glowy-eyed demon resided within their friend.

"She better not puke neon goo in the back of my new car," Eve groaned and shut the trunk.

Chapter Fourteen

Tina and Eve drove to the old church cemetery in silence as a full moon followed them overhead. Tina's body trembled as they pulled into the cemetery, afraid that they would not be able to undo what they had unleashed. It was true that she loved Lacey as more than just a friend, but at that moment, none of that mattered. All she wanted was for her friend to be okay, and for things to go back the way they were.

"Deon said that they would be waiting for us under the big banyan tree," Eve said, slowly driving through the cemetery. Rows and rows of headstones illuminated in the twin headlights, and Tina shivered at the thought of so many bodies buried right there beneath their feet.

So many memories, so many people loved and lost, now gone forever.

Eve parked near the old banyan tree by an outcrop of mausoleums and killed the headlights. Sure enough, two shadowy figures loomed at the twisted root base of the massive tree. Tina hitched her backpack over her shoulder as she and Eve exited the car. The two shadowy figures approached under the silvery moonlight as banyan leaves crunched under their boots.

"Did you bring her?" Deon asked.

"Yeah, she's in the trunk," Eve said. "We put a binding spell on her wrist."

"Are you sure you did it right?" The other teen who must have been Ras emerged from the shadows. Like his namesake, Rasputin had long, dark scraggly hair and the beginnings of a patchy beard. His eyes were rimmed in black eyeliner and silver rings adorned his fingers. Like Deon and Eve, he was outfitted in the finest black fishnet and pleather mall goth ensemble that their small town had to offer.

"Yes, we did it right!" Eve hissed. "Ras, I should kick your ass for putting us in this situation in the first place!"

"Me! I wasn't the one stupid enough to play with a

spirit board," Ras snorted. "Hurry up, the altar is all set. We need to do this thing before the candles burn out."

Eve popped her trunk and she and Tina hauled Lacey's limp body toward the altar. A warm hairdryer breeze kicked up, and Tina's gut lurched again.

"Eve," she said. "We better hurry."

Deon and Ras had drawn a pentagram with chalk on a slab of concrete in front of the mausoleum. Black candles were lit at each point of the star, their flames flickering in the warm late summer breeze. The two friends gently laid Lacey in the center of the star and stood back. Eve passed the leatherbound book to Ras as Tina opened her backpack.

"You brought the spirit board, right?"

Tina nodded and revealed the Ouija board.

"Put it on the ground, there, next to her body," Ras nodded toward the ground. "If this works, the demon will leave your friends' body and return to the spirit board."

"What do you need us to do?" Eve asked.

Ras flipped through the book and landed on a page near the end. He handed Eve the book and pointed. "See right here? You both have to chant this passage until the demon leaves."

"What happens if the demon doesn't leave?" Tina asked.

Ras shrugged. "I don't know. I've never done this before."

"Great." Eve huffed. "Okay, let's give this a try then."

"Here," Deon said. "I think you dropped this."

Tina glanced at Deon and the pit in her stomach opened wider. Her legs grew weak as she grasped the white scrunchie from his hand.

"Oh no ..."

Eve jabbed an elbow into Tina's ribs as a cry squeaked from her lips. "Look."

Lacey was no longer unconscious, lifeless and contained. Lacey was *floating*. Her eyes glowed like two flashlights in the dark as she hovered in a vertical stance just a foot above the pentagram. Rows of razor sharp teeth filled her mouth again as the terrible sound of demonic laughter filled the air.

"What the hell, Ras?" Eve shouted. "This isn't supposed to happen! We're on hallowed ground!"

"This isn't a church cemetery," Deon said. "It's just a public cemetery."

"This is why children shouldn't play with witchcraft," Lacey chuckled in her demonic voice. "They never pay attention to important details."

"Read the passage!" Ras said. "Don't let her distract you!"

"Not very smart, are you?" The demon opened her mouth wide to reveal her rows of sharp teeth. Ras let out a yelp and tried to back away, but he was too late. Lacey released a violent, torrential stream of glowing green goo all over the would-be wizard.

"Eve! We have to read!" Tina hissed.

"Okay, okay. It's here," Eve said. "What was done, now undo. *Quod factum est, nunc perdes.*"

"Tina, look out!" Deon pushed the two teens to the ground as a wooden bench whizzed through the air. The book was knocked from Eve's hands as the two friends hit the floor. The demon Lacey cackled with her hands raised in the air, her fingers gnarled and twisted. A planter full of tropical flowers that had been next to the bench levitated, and the demon moved its hands as if guiding it through the air.

"Flower delivery!" The demon cackled as the planter whizzed through the air. The planter hit Deon in the center of his back, knocking him to the ground.

"Eve! We've got to hurry!" Tina picked up the book, her hands trembling as she struggled to find the page.

The demon yawned. "Your little attempts at conjuring have been fun, but I'm growing tired of this game."

"Here!" Tina said, pointing to the page. "I found it. *Quod factum est, nunc perdes.*"

"Oof." The demon lowered its hands and doubled over. The Ouija board trembled on the ground and a low moan filled the air.

"Oh my gosh," Eve said. "I think it's working! Say it again."

"*Quod factum est, nunc perdes,*" Tina said again. This time, the earth trembled under their feet.

"You little witch!" The demon shrieked, still doubled over. "Stop this nonsense!"

"It's working," Deon said, still crouched on the ground. "Keep going."

"High school is so overrated," the demon said. "Be my slave instead. You can have all of the clothes and friends and fun you want. Every day will be a trip to the mall, a day at the arcade. The perfect slumber party from hell!"

"Never!" Tina shouted. "Quod factum est, nunc perdes!"

"Tiny!" Lacey's voice cried out. The light left her eyes, and the atmosphere no longer supported her. Her body crumpled to the ground as though the rug had been pulled out from underneath her.

"Lacey!" Tina dropped the book and ran to her side.

"No!" Eve shouted.

Tina kneeled by her friend's body and cradled her head in her hands. Her eyes were closed, and her body was limp. Her skin was cold to the touch. At peace.

"Please don't leave us, Lacey," Tina sobbed. A hot tear rolled down her cheek. "We need you to come back. I love you so much."

The tear dropped from Tina's cheek as she sobbed. It splashed down on Lacey's cheek. Her eyes flew open. Glowing eyes.

"She'll never love you!" The demon cackled.

"Hold her!" Ras shouted.

"Quod factum est, nunc perdes."

"Quod factum est, nunc perdes."

"Quod factum est, nunc perdes."

"Quod factum est, nunc perdes."

"Quod factum est, nunc perdes."

"Quod factum est, nunc perdes."

"Quod factum est, nunc perdes."

"Quod factum est, nunc perdes."

Eve and Deon chanted the incantation over and over

again as Tina sat at the center of the pentagram and held onto her best friend. Lacey's face contorted and gurgled as a hot wind whipped around them in a tornado frenzy. She stared at her friends' face illuminated in the moonlight and cried as the demon fought to stay inside.

"Quod factum est, nunc perdes."

"Quod factum est, nunc perdes."

"Quod factum est, nunc perdes."

"Quod factum est, nunc perdes."

"Quod factum est, nunc perdes."

"Quod factum est, nunc perdes."

"Quod factum est, nunc perdes."

"Quod factum est, nunc perdes."

"You ... cannot ... contain ... me ..." the demon said, the glow in its eyes fading. A final warm breeze blew through the cemetery, extinguishing the flames and blowing away the salt circle pentagram. Lacey's body quivered and convulsed one final time as the Ouija board trembled beside her. And then, as quickly as it began, the ceremony was over.

"Did it work?" Eve asked.

"Is she dead?" Deon peered out from behind Eve.

Tina placed a kiss on Lacey's forehead.

Lacey opened her eyes. "Uh, what's going on?"

"Lacey!" Tina sobbed and scooped her friend into a hug. "I thought you were gone!"

"Oh, thank goodness!" Eve pushed Deon aside and wrapped Tina and Lacey in a hug.

"I had the weirdest dream," Lacey said. "We were all trapped in a dARiA*s catalog."

"Yeah, I know," Tina laughed, wiping tears from her eyes. "Lacey, I'm so sorry."

"Are we in a cemetery?" Lacey sat up and glanced around. "Is that Tyler? Why are you covered in a bunch of Nickelodeon slime?"

"I go by Rasputin now," he said, wiping gunk from his beard.

Eve stood and held out her hand to help Lacey up. "We'll explain it all on the way home."

"We're sorry we accidentally got you possessed."

Eve and Tina stood outside of Lacey's front door later that evening covered in cemetery dirt and green slime remnants. The infected scratch on Eve's arm seemed to have calmed down, and besides a few bruises, Lacey seemed no worse for the wear. It was almost as if the events of the sleepover had never even happened.

"I still don't know what to think," Lacey said, tucking a strand of hair behind one ear. "I don't remember anything."

"That's probably for the best," Eve said. "One things' for sure, I'm done messing with witchcraft."

"And Ouija boards," Tina snorted.

"What did you do with the one at the cemetery?" Eve asked.

"Oh, it was gone," Tina said. "I figured Deon or Ras picked it up."

"That's okay. I didn't really want it back." Eve crossed her arms in front of her chest and gazed at Lacey. "So, you're really okay?"

"Totally fine." Lacey shrugged her shoulders. "I'm sorry your birthday party sleepover was ruined."

Tina smiled. "I have my two best friends back. That's all that matters."

"Group hug!" Eve scooped Tina and Lacey into her arms. The three friends embraced on Lacey's front porch in a circle, just like they used to. Best friends forever.

"It's late and my folks are going to kill me if I don't

get home soon," Eve said, breaking away. "We'll see you in school tomorrow?"

Lacey nodded. "Definitely."

"We'll see you there," Tina said, leaning in for one last hug.

Lacey waited on her front porch and waved as Eve and Tina pulled out of her driveway. Tina kept her eyes locked on her best friend until they turned the corner and she couldn't see her anymore. "Pick you up for school tomorrow?" Eve asked as she dropped Tina off.

"Yeah," Tina nodded. "I would like that."

"Don't let the bedbugs bite," Eve said, and rolled up the window.

Tina waited and watched her friend drive away into the night, musing on the way the tides had turned. She was sixteen. Everything was different now. Tomorrow would be the first day of tenth grade, and she had conquered her worst fears. She told Lacey she loved her and she didn't die. Yes, they did accidentally evoke a demon, but that's what sleepover birthday parties are for, right?

As she showered, brushed her teeth and got ready for bed that night, Tina counted herself lucky. She didn't know what the future would bring, but she did know one thing. Friends come and go, but best friends are there to stay. Tina and Lacey and Eve. Together forever.

Epilogue

The first day of tenth grade felt much like the first day of ninth grade to Tina; completely unremarkable. Tina dressed for school in the dark that morning, slipping in a new pair of button-fly jeans and a sunflower print t-shirt. Even though she was exhausted from the events of the weekend and not in the least excited about school, she was definitely looking forward to seeing her friends. Her mother was still asleep as she grabbed a Pop Tart and headed out into the dawn to find Eve waiting in her driveway.

"Did you have any weird dreams?" Eve asked as Tina slid into the passenger seat.

"No. Did you?"

"Yeah, I did," Eve said, throwing her car into reverse. "I dreamed we were back in the catalog again."

"Yikes," Tina said. "No one will ever believe what happened over the weekend, you know."

"Nope," Eve said. "I'm not going to tell anyone. Are you?"

"Nope," Tina said. "Do you think Lacey is really okay?"

Eve shrugged. "She looked okay to me. I wouldn't be surprised if there are long-lasting psychological repercussions to being possessed by a demon though."

"Not exactly something you can tell the school counselor is it?" Tina said. "I still feel bad."

"Lacey will forgive us," Eve said. "She has to. We're best friends."

Eve parked in the student lot outside of their school and the two girls got out. It was surprisingly quiet for the first day of school, though Eve had a habit of running late.

"Hey, is that Lacey?" Eve said, pulling her beeper from her pocket.

Sure enough, Lacey was standing outside of the school waiting for them like a beacon of light. Despite the fact that an ancient entity had taken over her body for most of the weekend, she looked pretty good; great, in fact. Her hair was sleek and glossy, her eyes bright and shining. Her smooth, deep tan had returned and she looked preppy, pretty and put together in her back-to-school floral dress. Tina's heart swelled as they approached and greeted each other with a hug.

"How are you feeling today?" Tina asked.

"Excellent," Lacey said. "Excited for the first day of school."

The girls walked to their lockers, the same ones they had the year before. Tina had made certain to reserve her usual locker right next to Lacey's over the summer. She turned the lock and opened the door to store her backpack. Taped to the inside of the locker door was the photo of her and Lacey and Eve when they were in second grade. Someone had gouged out all of the eyes and made a rip through photo, separating Lacey from her two best friends.

"My pager isn't working," Eve turned away, smacking the side of the rectangular plastic case. "Lace, did you get my page this morning?"

Tina's stomach dropped. Something was very, very wrong.

"Oh, it's not Lacey anymore," she said. "I'm going to

go by Zoey from now on."

A hair dryer warm wind blew across the campus and a swirl of notebook paper billowed at their feet. It was then that Tina realized the hallways looked different from before. Less decorated. More ... white.

"Eve." Tina whispered, tugging at her friend's sleeve. "Are you seeing this?"

Eve looked up from her pager and gasped. The kids in the hall were all dressed fashionably in bucket hats, snowboard sweaters, baby tee's and oversized jeans. A girl in cloud print pajamas did cartwheels down the hall, as another girl giggled and hiked up her denim skirt to show off a pair of pink boots to her friend. There was one decoration on the wall though, a single sign hung over the cafeteria. Tina read it and her heart dropped.

wELcOmE bAcK sTuDeNtS

"Tina." Eve whispered. "Are we ..."

Lacey, or rather, Zoey, closed her locker door and flipped her perfect blonde hair over her shoulder. She gazed out at the school campus and gave a nod of approval. "You know, they say high school is hell. I think I'll feel right at home here."

Tina's legs grew weak. Their incantation had failed. Her best friend was really and truly gone. She grabbed

Eve's arm to steady herself as their friend turned away and sauntered off down the hall. They watched her, stunned in silence, unable to warn the rest of the school about what kind of terror they accidentally unleashed. Tina cocked her head to the side as she spotted something sticking out of her demonic friend's backpack at an unnatural angle. Something that looked an awful lot like a board game. Lacey's sneakers didn't even seem to touch the ground as she disappeared into the crowd.

Acknowledgements

This book wouldn't be possible without the works of R.L. Stine, Christopher Pike, Lois Lowery, Anne M. Martin, Lois Duncan and Alvin Schwartz. As a young reader, I devoured their stories and, in turn, was inspired to become an author myself. Thank you for giving dreamy, spooky young readers like me a reason to read under the covers late at night.

Thank you to *Are You Afraid of the Dark?*, *Eerie Indiana*, *Tales From the Crypt*, *Candyman*, *Scream*, *Pumpkinhead*, *Clueless*, *Ouija Boards*, Blockbuster Video, Doritos Cool Ranch, Dr. Pepper, and of course, *dELiA*s* for shaping my teens and my love of all things pink horror and 90s adjacent.

Thank you to my family, friends, readers and fellow authors for being in my corner. I wouldn't have the courage to do this without your support!

About the Author

Wendy Dalrymple loves to explore the beauty in horrific things. When she's not writing femme-focused horror, you can find her hiking with her family, painting (bad) wall art, and trying to grow as many pineapples as possible.

Follow her on Instagram and TikTok:
@wendydalrymplewrites

TOTALLY FREAKED!

Did you love
Birthday Party Demon
by Wendy Dalrymple?

Then don't miss
the next exciting
tale in the TOTALLY FREAKED!
series releasing
this summer!

CODESKULL
by
Chloe Spencer

Drawing inspiration from classic video games, *CodeSkull* centers on an ambitious arcade gamer, Mick, who is one day gifted a CD of an RPG game by her rival, Tommy. But when she plays it, she inadvertently unleashes a **TERRIFYING TECHNOLOGICAL CREATURE** that can infest and overload any electrically powered object.

After their classmate meets a grisly end, the two must team up with a fledgling occult enthusiast in order to save their small town-and possibly the world-from annihilation...

Paperback ISBN: 978-1-966497-00-4
eBook ISBN: 978-1-966497-01-1

www.ingramcontent.com/pod-product-compliance
Lightning Source LLC
Chambersburg PA
CBHW061544310726
48972CB00008B/2608